Tucker McBride

and the *Christmas Gift*

Doris Gaines Rapp

Doris Gaines Rapp, Ph.D.

Tucker McBride

and the *Christmas Gift*

Daniel's House Publishing - Huntington, Indiana

In cooperation with Never Alone Publishing
Fort Wayne, Indiana

Name: Doris Gaines Rapp, Ph.D.
Title: Tucker McBride and the Christmas Gift

Library of Congress Control Number: 2024904491

Identifiers:
ISBN: (paperback) 979-8-9885283-1-9
ISBN: (eBook) 979-8-9885283-2-6

Cover design is stock imagery from @Dreamstime.com. (ID 101661817) Put in place by @Debi Lindhorst/The Type Galley, Warren, Indiana. Other images are drawings or pictures of antiques.

All Scripture quotations, unless otherwise indicated, are taken from the Holy Bible, New International Version®, NIV®. Copyright ©1973, 1978, 1984, 2011 by Biblica, Inc.™ Used by permission of Zondervan. All rights reserved worldwide. www.zondervan.comThe "NIV" and "New International Version" are trademarks registered in the United States Patent and Trademark Office by Biblica, Inc.™

website: www.dorisgainesrapp.com
contact: dorisgainesrapp@gmail.com

Tucker McBride was an adventurous kid, one who rarely thought before he acted. Learn from Tucker. Do not try Tucker's stunts.

Glossary
For an unfamiliar word with an asterisk (*) beside it, go to the back of the book for a definition or picture.

Published by Daniel's House Publishing - Huntington, Indiana
in cooperation with Never Alone Publishing - Fort Wayne, Indiana

Daniel's House Publishing - Huntington, Indiana

In cooperation with Never Alone Publishing - Fort Wayne, Indiana

Acknowledgments

A big "Thank you" to all my dear writer friends in our group, Inspiration Inc. Your positive encouragement is a real blessing. I have learned so much from all of you.

I want to thank Kim Autrey, editor, and publisher at Never Alone Publishing, for all of her support and creative work. You continue to be positive and uplifting with your enthusiasm and expertise. Thanks, Kim.

Thanks to Donna Nehring who has been reading and supporting all of my books. Your suggestions are creative and welcomed. Thanks, Donna.

Thank you, Mark and Julie Blake. You two are the reason for *Tucker McBride and the Christmas Gift.* Your enthusiasm for all of my Tucker books, required a continuation of the series, due to your love of Tucker.

Thanks to Debi Lindhorst at the Type Galley in Warren, Indiana. I create the covers and you put them together. What would I do without you? I would have them polished off with scotch tape and white school paste. Thanks, Debi.

Tucker McBride

and the Christmas Gift

CONTENTS

In loving memory of my husband, Bill Rapp's

grandparents, Albert and Perninnah Kime.

After rearing their own five children,

their youngest, Helen Kime Rapp died.

Grandma and Grandpa Kime took in and

reared Helen's four children when

Gramma Kime was 67 and Grandpa Kime was 77.

The children were:

Jack – age 9

Beverly – age 7

Merry – age 3

Bill (Tucker McBride) – age 3 months.

Only love is that generous.

CHAPTER ONE

Six Days Before Christmas and Still No Gift

Friday, December 19, 1947

"Tucker McBride! We don't run in the halls," Principal Metzger bellowed.

Tucker thought, *We? Mr. Metzger, I didn't know you could still run.* He decided it was best not to bring up the principal's lack of zip.

That afternoon, Tucker was excited. The extra energy in his legs demanded that he bolt down the school hallway. Instead, a speedy walk would have kept him out of trouble. With his muscles taut, it looked like he was in the starting blocks of the hundred-yard dash. But it wasn't a track meet. Getting Christmas vacation started as soon as possible was his only event. And the excitement had nothing to do with receiving fancy-wrapped presents. His frenzied fuss was in anticipation of the holiday freedom that lay just beyond the side door of the middle school. No more confines of school, just the open spaces that stretched for miles in and around Dunlap, Indiana. His energy was fired up by the possibility of earning money for Gramma's surprise Christmas present.

As Tucker neared the door and freedom, Principal Metzger stood rigidly against the wall with his arms folded. He looked like a member of the Royal Foot Guard just inside the palace. When Tucker saw the principal watching his every step, he was careful that his fast footfalls could not be classified as running. He quickly stepped off the fastest heel-toe waddle Tucker had ever performed. It was the end of the last day of school before Christmas vacation, and Tucker was not going to spend one second in after-school detention. There was still way too much to do. Fearing he'd be late for work; he was determined that wouldn't happen.

"Have a great Christmas vacation, Tucker." Mr. Metzger's deep voice rumbled from where he stood, along the side of the hall like the Captain of the Guard.

Tucker started to speak then pulled in his chin and lowered his pitch. "You, too, Mr. Metzger." Tucker smiled. Though only fourteen, his voice already sounded deeper than many of the other boys.

Amazingly, the junior high school halls still smelled of pine needles from the Christmas trees that decorated each classroom. The festive evergreens had been up for weeks. However, as he got closer to the door, the evergreen perfume competed with the not-so-pleasant aroma of the half peanut butter and jelly sandwich that lay on the floor. It had been stomped on by several size twelves by the time the upperclassmen had cleared out of the building.

Tucker slid past Mrs. Hunter's history class, with its red and green paper chain swagged above the door. A cold blast of icy air from outside hit him in the face. The door constantly flew open as streams of students dashed out. The winter afternoon high was only twenty-five degrees. Northern Indiana could surprise you with almost any kind of weather. Gramma always said that an Indiana December had six seasons: (1) lingering autumn, (2) introduction to winter, (3) fake winter, (4) spring's return, (5) double-cross frigid air, and (6) six feet of snow.

Tucker pulled his tan, buckskin suede jacket more tightly around him. Sam Treadway had given him the deerskin coat and Tucker prized it.

Sam, Gramma's cousin, had moved out west to Colorado after his wife died. He left his farm and Indiana behind him. Still, he had to revisit the Midwest from time to time, to wrap himself in the love of family. Tucker breathed in the mountain-man scent of his sleeve, inhaling the earthy sweet aroma of the leather.

Sam was amazed by the poor fit of Tucker's previous outerwear. The boy had grown so much during the first semester of eighth grade, that his former coat fit him like he'd rolled down the steps, toes-over-tea kettle, and got trapped inside a straight-jacket. Sam said he figured the boy needed the jacket more than he did. Sam just wore it by habit. Now that he had been staying with the Moyers, away from the wind and blizzards of the western mountains, a farm jacket would be best. And cloth wouldn't attract Indiana's foxtail weeds like the leather did.

Tucker's friend, Gilbert, stood by the door, blowing the three-note repetition of the song, "Jingle Bells," on his trumpet. Then he paused and completed the first two measures with three more b's. Startled by the horn's blast, Anna Frederick screamed. Her piercing cry added more to the chaos of the end-of-day routine than the horn.

"Gilbert!" Mr. Metzger shouted. "Put that away!"

Anna still had her hands cupped to her ears. She always overreacted, or to Tucker's mind, over-acted. She slipped into her Miss Woe character whenever anyone shifted attention away from her. Gilbert certainly had. When Anna yelled out, Tucker saw Gilbert smile and mouth, "My job is done." Gilbert opened his horn case and smiled as he put it inside.

Tucker couldn't get past Mrs. Hunter's history classroom door fast enough. Not because he didn't like Mrs. Hunter. She was his favorite teacher. And, he would have stopped to talk to her for who knows how long. But he had promised Butch Randolf at the Sinclair gas station, that he would work an hour or two after school. The station was across the road in front of the Moyer's home. It was easy to help out. Besides, Tucker needed the money, with Christmas gliding up on a red sleigh.

Outside the school, snow still lay on the ground from the two-day fall of white crystals earlier that week. Frozen alley stones crunched under his feet. As Tucker hurried along, the ground cover of ice couldn't mask the approaching footsteps behind him.

"Tucker, slow down." Christy Tree jogged up behind him, slipping and sliding on the gravel.

"Sorry, I have to hurry, Christy." Tucker reached down and scratched the silky head of his dog, Joe who ran up to greet him at the gate. True, the shepherd was a family member. But when the decorated war dog returned from the great battle, he chose to stick to Gramma's or Tucker's side.

"What's the big hurry?" Christy stopped at Moyers' sleeping garden and leaned on the alley gate.

Tucker shrugged and stepped into the backyard where he and his brother and two sisters lived with their grandparents. "I don't have enough money for Gramma's present yet. Butch said I could work for him for a few hours today. I want to get something to eat first."

Christy stared at the frosty ground. "Does that mean the Christmas dance at the school is out?"

Tucker stopped and stroked his chin. "That's this evening, isn't it?"

"Yep. Mama bought me a new, red taffeta dress and black shoes with a little heel."

Tucker's mind whirled. "Is everyone going?" He thought of all the kids from his Sunday school class. He and Christy had been close to all of them since everyone attended the nursery class in the room with the big window overlooking the sanctuary. It was a very small community. Those were also the same people he saw at school every day. The entire eighth-grade class at Concord Middle School only numbered seventy-seven students.

"Everyone," Christy echoed. "I just saw Freddie in the hallway, and he said he was going too. You know Freddie Cooper. He's the last person to go to something like that."

"I'll be at Butch's until supper at 5:30," Tucker processed. "I can eat fast, clean up, and change by...6:30."

Christy shook her head in disbelief. "Do you chew or inhale your food?"

"Inhale." Tucker moved in through the yard, then turned. "Do you want to walk up here, or should I come down and we'll walk to school from your house?"

"I'll come up here," Christy called after him. "Then you can walk me home when the dance is over, and it's darker outside."

"Sounds good," Tucker called over his shoulder as he kept going. Then, he added with a chuckle, "Better wear boots. You'll fall flat on all of that taffeta, wearing those fancy black shoes."

They made a good plan, but would Tucker be able to finish what he started for Gramma's Christmas present? The family often thought he didn't finish his projects. "Fumble-fingers," his brother, Tim, often called him. "Always dropping the ball." But then, Tim teased everyone about everything. Still, Tim was away in the Marine Corps. It would be Tucker's first Christmas without his whole family at home. The house was still full. Grandpop's cousin Sarah had moved in after her husband, Steven, died. She was staying in Tim's room while he was in the military. And, Sam Treadway had been sleeping on the couch for the last two months.

Tucker had six days until Christmas. He had a lot of work to do if he was going to give Gramma the gift he had in mind. Near the back of the house, he hurried past the huge underground root cellar. He thought about pulling a couple of carrots from the many varieties of vegetables that were stored there. The pit beneath the ground was covered in a white blanket of snow. *Getting some rabbit food out of the root cellar will take more time than grabbing something from the kitchen,* he mumbled. *I'll have to be careful. Gramma said she was going to bake today. She'll guard her Christmas cookies with a rolling pin in her hand.*

"I'm home," Tucker called as he popped through the summer house door and darted up a few steps into the kitchen. The entire house smelled like the sugar and butter of Gramma's famous cut-out holiday cookies.

"Ja, Tucker." His tiny, 4-foot 10-and-a-half-inch grandmother stood at the kitchen door with her tired hand gripping the doorknob. "I hope I'm not making a mistake. I set aside three cookies to hold you over 'til supper. Betsy said something about a Christmas dance at the school. She thought you were going."

"I am. Christy and I plan to walk together." Tucker eyed the large dishpan on the counter.

The pan was covered with a tea towel with a Christmas bell embroidered at the bottom. He knew the iced sugar cookies were under the cloth. They always were Gramma put the holiday cookies in a dish pan large enough for the icing not to touch until it was hard.

"Now, Tucker, you daresn't get into the cookies I've already baked and stored. They're for the church Christmas party and our family celebration." Gramma's tone was soft, but firm. "I left out an iced bell, a decorated Christmas tree, and a colorful sugary ornament for you."

Grandpop came up from behind Gramma, put his hands on her shoulders as if he were on her side, and then winked at Tucker. "The problem isn't one cookie now and then, Tucker. With your appetite, it's that the whole pan of cookies could be gone while you're deciding what you want to eat next."

"Got ya, Grandpop. I promise." Tucker crossed his chest with a large X over his heart. "I'll only eat the ones Gramma gives me." Tucker slipped off his jacket and draped it over the back of a dining room chair before bounding up the stairs, two steps at a time.

He tossed his school three-ring binder and his other books on his bed. Leaping back down the steps like a paratrooper jumping from an airplane, he made a perfect landing on the front hall hardwood floor. Careful not to run through the house, he hurried back to collect his jacket, then started toward the door. "I'm going over to work at Butch's station for a while before dinner. If I work some of my vacation hours, I'll have enough money to buy the stuff I want."

"Slow down a little, Tucker," Grandpop warned. "The newsboys are still on the porch, folding their bag of papers."

"And newsgirls," Tucker's older sister Betsy called out as she started up the steps.

The *Elkhart Truth* had dropped off bundles of the evening's newspapers on the Moyer front porch every day for years. Neighborhood boys and girls gathered there to count and fold the papers they would toss onto front porches on their news route. Tucker would have to step over or around them on his way to work.

"Here's your cookies." Gramma handed him the three large sugar cookies wrapped in a clean, cloth napkin. "Now, ya daresn't leave the napkin in the dirty service bay. The napkin is old, but it's still usable."

"I'll bring it home, Gramma."

"What stuff are you wanting to *buy*, Tucker?" Grandpop asked as he helped with his jacket. Tucker's hands were full of cookies.

"I haven't finished buying Christmas presents." Tucker fastened his jacket with one hand as he hurried toward the door.

"No need to spend much money," Grandpop reminded Tucker in his usual frugal way.

Tucker checked the clock on the wall and nearly ran toward the door.

"My gracious," Gramma gasped with her hand to her chest. "Just watching that boy move through the house, makes me tired."

"Okay, Grandpop," Tucker agreed as he reached for the door handle. "I'll see you later." Tucker didn't argue with his grandparents. Don't misunderstand. He didn't always agree either. He just smiled and quietly went about doing what he had planned all along.

CHAPTER TWO

"Work" – Definition: Getting Paid to Have Fun

Butch Randolf's service station smelled like Pennzoil and Ethel gasoline. That was perfume to Tucker's senses. It was a manly aroma that clung to his hair and clothes long after he left the place.

Tucker opened the door to the station's office where customers settled their weekly gasoline bill, bought extra cans of oil for long trips, and purchased chips and other snacks. Tucker burned a straight path to the caramel, peanuts, and fudge-filled PowerHouse candy bars. He carefully placed the napkin-covered cookies on the display case and slid the door open from behind. Ripping the wrapper off a candy bar, he inhaled the creamy chocolate. Reaching into his pocket, he pulled out three nickels. Like an orchestra conductor with graceful, fluid movements, he completed his candy overture by snatching up a Zagnut peanut butter candy bar and an Oh Henry. He slipped the bars into his pocket to eat as soon as the PowerHouse hit his stomach. He swallowed the caramel and peanuts with his teeth scarcely sinking into the fudgy scrumptiousness. The sugary sweetness of it all raised his energy enough to hear Butch in the workspace through another door.

Butch was in the bay area, working on Mrs. Hunter's Chevy sedan. She would hurry catty-cornered across the street from the school any minute with a long list of errands to run. She'd need her car. Butch never wanted to make a customer wait.

"What do you want me to do, Butch?" Tucker called toward the attached garage with a mouth full of candy. "The wash bay will be cold, but I'll be happy to wash cars for you."

Butch took a red work cloth from his hip pocket and wiped his hands. "Nah, Tucker, thanks. I really need you out on the drive. I have to finish this Chevy. Then I have two more minor repair jobs on those cars out back. I'm stuck in here. I can't pump gas. Do you want our customers to have to pump their own gas?"

"We can't have that, Butch." Tucker grinned as he started back outside.

"Hold on," Butch stopped Tucker and pointed to the wall behind the door. "Get that old jacket of mine hanging on the hook. The coat you're wearing is a mighty nice one. You don't want to get gasoline on it." Butch started back out to the wrench he left under the Chevy's hood just as the bell on the drive rang.

Tucker took the clean but stained coat from the wall hook and hung up his own. He was still putting his arm into the left sleeve of the jacket with "Butch's Sinclair" painted in an arch on the back when he swallowed the last bite of his first bar. Tucker stepped back as Principal Metzger pulled into a parking space on the side of the drive.

Tucker zipped up the jacket just as Metzger got out of his car. Tucker asked, "Did you lock the school door, Mr. Metzger?"

"The janitors will secure the building when they leave in a while." Metzger stepped into the office. "I stopped off to pay my bill, Tucker. Is it okay with Butch if I leave the money with you?"

"That's fine," Butch called from the adjoining bay.

"Here you are." Metzger removed his wallet from his hip pocket and pulled out a ten and a five-dollar bill. "My gas bill is twelve dollars and fifty cents."

Tucker picked up the receipt book that lay beside the cash register and quickly wrote down the amount. "Here you go," he offered after taking the change from the drawer. "Two dollars and fifty cents change."

"Thanks, Tucker." The principal reached over the counter and patted Tucker on the shoulder. "You did that very professionally."

Tucker's eyes popped. "I just remembered something. Is the school going to be open tomorrow?"

"The last day of school was today," Metzger reminded him as he started to leave.

"Right," Tucker agreed. But to himself, his attitude was sharper. *You did it again. You didn't complete your job. You left half of Gramma's present at the school.* He wanted to call after Mr. Metzger as the principal left the station and got into his car. But he knew it wasn't Metzger's fault. Tucker was in too big of a hurry earlier to get the holiday break started and burst out of the school without thinking.

"Hey, Tucker," Vinny Wagoner shouted out the driver's side window of his four-door crimson red Plymouth with a grey top. Vinny talked about his car all the time. He bragged that his dad gave it to him when Mr. Wagoner bought a new Chrysler. Vinny spoke to Tucker in a low, confidential tone. "Looks like Butch is busy. You got any cigars in the office?" The terrible threesome grinned in unison. Morty was in the front passenger seat and Gus sat in the back.

Tucker shook his head and thought, *it's like they have assigned seats.* Then, he reminded the trio, "You know I can't sell you guys any cigars. Besides, you've been coming to church and Sunday school, Vinny. What has Birdie Kline said about smoking?"

Morty leaned in Tucker's direction. "You know he only comes to church because your grandmother blackmailed him."

"Blackmailed?" Tucker sputtered as he felt his fists and jaws tighten.

"Hey," Vinny snapped, "knock it off, Mortimer. Mrs. Moyer is a good lady."

"If she didn't blackmail you," Morty began, "how come you kept going to church after your deal with the old lady was up?"

"Old lady?" Tucker stepped toward the car as his fists tightened again.

"Haven't you noticed?" Morty asked with a sassy laugh.

Vinny gave Morty a soft punch in the arm. "Shut up, Morty."

Tucker glanced toward the open bay door. He saw Butch pull his head from under the hood of the Chevy and look out to the drive. Tucker lowered his voice and smiled like any good service attendant. "Morty, I noticed you're a pimple-faced loudmouth who doesn't know when to keep his mouth shut." He smiled again, using the customer-is-always-right attitude Butch insisted on. "You want me to ask Butch if he'd stop working and sell you one of the cheap stink bomb cigars? Course, your dad might hear about that."

"Never mind, Tucker," Morty growled.

To Morty, Vinny added, "Knock it off." He revved the engine, causing the souped-up car's tailpipes to belch. Before pulling off the station drive, he smiled at Tucker. "Tell that little pint-size grandmother of yours, Vinny said, Merry Christmas." His eyes focused on the large steering wheel. "I never really knew what Christmas was all about before she forced me into coming to your church after that Halloween incident. She stands ten feet tall in my book."

Tucker stood back from the car and nodded. "I'll tell her, Vinny."

Vinny steered the loud hotrod, with gold flames painted on the sides, back onto the highway. As he pulled away, he waved his hand out the window, low down where the other guys wouldn't be able to see his friendly gesture.

Tucker shook his head and thought, *Grandpop had a good name for you guys—Dummkopfs*. Vinny had no more than pulled away when Tucker turned to find Gladys Rinker's car waiting at the pump. "Yes, Ma'am. Fill 'er up?" He popped another bite of candy into his mouth.

"Just three dollars, Tucker." Gladys began wringing her hands. "I still have to go back to that mechanic George told me about, Dan Moppet. Mr. Moppet said I needed a new master thingamabob on the output manifold."

Tucker nearly choked on his last half-bite of chocolate as he stifled a laugh. "That's what he called it,

Mrs. Rinker, a master thingamabob on the output manifold? Or, is that what you called it?"

"No, not me," she gulped. The pitch of her voice rose in frantic confusion. "I have no idea what's under the hood. The car just kept making a chugging sound. That's what Mr. Moppet called it, the thingamabob."

"Yes, Ma'am." Tucker replaced the gas cap and wiped his hands. "Mrs. Rinker, I hate to tell you this, but there is no master thingamabob for the output manifold. Dan was joking with you."

"What? Oh, thank you, Tucker," she said as she breathed deeply. "I can't afford a master thingamabob. Dan said it would be really expensive." She looked out the windshield. "I wonder how much they cost."

"Like I said, Mrs. Ricker...." Then he stopped when it was obvious that he wasn't really reaching her. "I'll check if Butch has time to look at your car," Tucker offered.

"Well, never mind." Gladys hung her head as she took a five-dollar bill from her purse. "George said not to worry about it."

"Well, if your car is making a lot of noise, it should be fixed," Tucker began, trying to be helpful. He pulled two dollars from the roll of bills he kept in his pocket and handed her the change. "Two dollars, Ma'am."

"George said, the other day when it snowed so hard, our cat got up inside the car and curled up on the engine to get warm. She's mostly an outside cat." Pulling a handkerchief from her coat pocket, she blew her nose. "George said, when he ran to the drug store to get my medication, he didn't know that Rhubarb, that's our cat, was still snuggled up to the sparkplugs. When the car revved up, and the fan belt flew around, George heard a loud yowling. But I didn't believe him. Cats don't do that, do they?"

"I can't say I know," Tucker admitted behind a well-hidden smile. "Is Rhubarb alright?" he asked. Tucker figured the cat would look a fright if it had tangled with the massive engine of an automobile.

"Rhubarb did look nearly shaved to the skin on her left side." Mrs. Rinker blotted her eyes. "But I thought George was just telling me one of his stories. He loves to play pranks."

Tucker cleared his throat. "I imagine there's a lot of cat hair still under the hood." As he spoke, he turned and pretended to scratch his nose so Mrs. Rinker wouldn't see his broad smile. He knew it wasn't good business to laugh at the customers. "All that fuzzy stuff could clog the engine."

"Yes, Tucker. That's what George said." Gladys started the car and slowly pulled off the drive, chugging and spluttering out onto South Main Street.

Tucker hurried into the office holding his breath. Once inside, he laughed until he doubled over. When the drive bell sounded again, Tucker hurried out the door. He was still chuckling and wiping happy tears from his eyes as he greeted a valued customer. Tucker figured he had the best job around. Where else could he laugh and have fun while getting paid seventy-five cents an hour?

CHAPTER THREE

Plans for the Evening, Plans for Sunday,
and Plans for Tim

It was 5:35 when Tucker dashed up the front steps onto the wide front porch. A few small pieces of twine that had been cut from one of the bundles of newspapers were scattered under the wooden porch swing. Grandpop missed those when he gathered up the longer pieces to twist into a long rope. Tucker paused and looked in through the etched, oval glass of the front door. *Good,* he thought. *Looks like the family is starting to come to the table.* Tucker smiled as Sam Treadway, Gramma's cousin, pulled out a chair for Sarah Harter, Grandpop's cousin, on the other side of the family. Sam was sure acting funny for a rugged, outdoor man. Maybe his extended visit was turning him back into a Hoosier.

Tucker eased himself through the door, removed his coat, and hung it on the hall tree near the stairsteps. The house smelled like carrots, onions, and richly browned beef. Tucker knew one of Gramma's brown-topped loaves of yeasty homemade bread would be sliced and buttered to soak up the gravy-like broth. Then, since it was Friday, there would be homemade apple pie for dessert.

"Ah, ja, Tucker. Ist gut you are home. Supper's on." Gramma stretched up straighter with her hand on her hip, easing her sore back. "Wash your hands."

Tucker darted into the little bathroom a family friend constructed in the stairwell under the steps. Grabbing the bar of Lava soap, he scrubbed the oil and gasoline from the station off his hands before they touched Gramma's everyday Christmas tablecloth.

In the dining room, Tucker took his usual seat beside Grandpop. Gramma sat at the foot of the table, and the rest of the family took chairs on the sides. When Grandpop began the blessing, "Our kind Heavenly Father—" each family member reached out like a spiritual ballet to gently take the hand of the one beside them.

Tucker smiled. The prayer was always the same, but so was the strong belief beneath the words. When Tucker heard the "Amen," he reached for the dish in front of him to pass.

As the serving bowl came to her, Betsy spooned some carrots and potatoes onto her plate. "Tucker, are you going to the dance?"

"Dance?" Gramma's cousin Sarah asked. "That sounds like fun."

"The Christmas dance is special," Carolyn, Tucker's oldest sister, explained. "I remember that one when I was in middle school. "First, it's the last activity before school is out for the holidays. And second, almost all the kids go. You can wear a fancy party dress, or your everyday school clothes. No one cares. The sponsors want to make it an activity for the whole school."

"I heard most of the girls are going to wear fancy duds," Betsy added as the meat platter was passed to her. "Did you get a new frock, Tucker?" she teased.

"Why, yes," Tucker munched with a full mouth. "I took the bus into Elkhart and bought a blue taffeta at Ziesel's Department Store so Christy and I could dress alike."

Sam joined in the ruse. "I'm sure you'll look lovely." He stopped and drank some coffee. With a masked smile, he added, "Sarah bought a taffeta dress the other day."

"Ja, Sam?" Gramma turned quizzically, studying Sarah's face. "A fancy dress?"

"It's not real fussy," Sarah protested shyly. "There's just a little lace around the collar and cuffs."

"You going to the dance too, Sarah?" Uncle Jacob quizzed with a twinkle in his voice.

Those at the table stopped chewing for a moment. Jacob Moyer seldom joked. A quiet bachelor, he usually buried his thoughts in his *National Geographic* magazines. He nearly memorized one or two newspapers that came to the house, or one of the many books he borrowed each week from the library.

"The dance?" Sarah kept that train of conversation going. "No. My mama wouldn't let me out that late."

"She's going to attend a wedding soon," Sam offered before he popped a bite-size piece of chuck roast into his mouth.

Gramma looked from Sam to Sarah, puzzled. "Is the wedding around here?"

"Oh, yes, very close," Sarah answered as she put her cloth napkin to her mouth. "As close as right here, the Moyer corner."

Gramma was confused. She was Rebecca Moyer. Her lips curved up quizzically. "Huh?"

Tucker was puzzled. His grandparents were the Moyers. His own mother was a Moyer before she married. Their house was on the Moyer corner, but so was the church. Gramma Moyer knew every event that required musical accompaniment. She didn't seem to know anything about an upcoming wedding.

"Rebecca, Sarah and I," Sam began in the softest voice Tucker had ever heard come out of the mountain man's mouth. Sam's smile covered his face. "We, ah—"

"Oh, Rebecca, it's so wonderful," Sarah muffled a giggle. "Sam asked me to marry him."

Tucker nearly choked on a large, unchewed bite of potato. "Marry?" He coughed and sputtered.

The rest of the family around the table blurted out their one-note chorus. "Marry?"

Sam touched Sarah's hand. "Yes, marry. And Sarah said yes. We figured, since the decision was made, there's no point in waiting. Our sweet spouses died quite some time ago." He teared up a little as Tucker tried not to gag on the rest of Sam's love song. "And no one wants to be alone." Sam stopped as pink rose up from his collar and covered his face with a blush.

Is Sam getting sick? Is he running a fever? Tucker thought. He had never thought that the man who carried a brace of pistols, a rifle, and slept under an Indian chief's blank would ever blush, over…a girl.

Sarah squeezed Sam's hand. "We just don't know exactly where, or when, or how many guests to prepare for."

"Only that?" Carolyn asked. "It sounds like we have a wedding to plan. I'd love to help."

Carolyn, Tucker's oldest sister and a senior in high school, was in the beginning stages of planning her own wedding. *Bride* magazines were stacked on the nightstand beside her bed and the floor in her room. Between her homework, her job at the switchboard in the local telephone office, and the precious little time she had left to spend with her fiancé, wedding planning was usually done late at night.

Tucker shoved the last bite of potato in his mouth and jumped up from the table. He could have said he felt sick but thought it might hurt Sam's feelings. "Excuse me. I have to get ready for the dance. You folks can talk wedding stuff."

Carolyn added some sisterly advice. "Make sure your fingernails are clean. Stinky oil and smudges don't belong at a Christmas dance."

"Thanks, Carolyn," Tucker hollered over his shoulder. "I never would have thought of that."

"Wait a minute, Tucker," Gramma called after him before he could get farther than her voice could reach. "I got a letter from Tim this afternoon. He said he gets to come home for a few days at Christmas before he's deployed overseas."

Tucker stopped with his hand on the top of the newel post at the bottom of the stairs, his head cocked to the side in thought. "Yeah?" Tucker tried to sound enthused. "When does he get here? Where's he gonna sleep? All the beds and the couch are taken."

Tucker was glad his older brother was coming home from specialized training before leaving for Korea. A time for family would be great for Tim. But since Tim has been gone, Tucker discovered that he felt more free. He knew he wasn't going to give up his bed. He peered around the wall dividing the living room from the entry hall and waited for the answer.

"Oh, he knows we're full," Gramma offered as she broke off a slice of her bread. "He said he could sleep on the floor or down at Aunt Cora's house."

"Oh…" Tucker thought and felt guilty for being selfish with his bed and bedroom.

"Well, hurry on. He'll get in on Sunday. Your Uncle David will drive up to Chicago to pick him up at the airport. David wants you to ride along. He said he's been awful tired."

"Okay," Tucker agreed. A smile started to sneak across his face. He liked spending time with his Uncle David. Even though he and his family just lived seven miles away, with Uncle David's busy schedule pastoring a church in Elkhart and Tucker's heavy school, sports, and work schedule, they didn't see much of each other. David was Tucker's mom's closest brother, and he was special. Uncle David called his little sister, his twin. When Tucker's mom died and he, Tim, and his sisters moved in with Gramma and Grandpop, Uncle David had been around more.

As Tucker mounted the steps, two at a time, his stomach began to churn. He wanted to see Tim. But he was able to forget some of Tim's teasing and criticism since his brother left. Now what should he expect?

In the little bathroom, Tucker scrubbed all over with the gritty, pumice-gray, Lava soap. It was usually used for taking grime off deeply soiled hands. He checked his upper lip just in case a mustache was beginning to grow, but the hairs were too fine for microscopic inspection. He removed Grandpop's straight razor from its safe place on the bottom shelf of the medicine cabinet. Holding his nose out of the way with his left hand, he ran the sharp blade over his skin. When the dangerous instrument of manly grooming nicked his lip, he winced. Reaching for the small crystal rock hunk of alum, Tucker ran the stone over the tiny drop of blood, immediately stopping any second or third droplet from oozing out. He smiled when he saw his manly nick in the mirror while drying his face.

In minutes, he was dressed in gray pants and a cream-colored, cable-knit sweater. "Hope I don't get too hot with all that hopping and dancing," he mumbled aloud. Tucker flew down the steps, grabbed his coat off the hall tree, and reached for the doorknob. "Bye, see you later."

"What time is it over?" Gramma called after him.

"Eleven. I'll be home about 11:30." Tucker opened the door and stepped out into the crisp, December air. So much to look forward to, so much to dread, all covered in fancy wrapping paper and tied with a bow. Christmas with the family, a wedding in the future, and his brother home for the holidays. Why did it always seem like a special time like Christmas, had to be so complicated?

CHAPTER FOUR
All that Glitters is Christmas

Twinkling lights of red, green, and gold, flashed in a multitude of eyes as Tucker and Christy entered the middle school gymnasium. Sparkling garlands draped from the ceiling were also swagged around the refreshment and punch bowl tables. The small gym was hopping with kids all trying to dance to swing music. While most of their attempts were fuzzy representations of the popular triple steps, a few were pretty good. The cheerleaders were especially gifted with the lifts, spins, and flips.

Tucker stopped cold at the entrance and stared. "I can't do that."

Christy rolled her eyes and pulled him into the room. "At least, help me with my coat."

"Can't you get it off," Tucker teased.

"Of course, I can," she snapped. "Tucker, helping a lady with her coat is the gentlemanly thing to do."

"Am I a gentleman, Christy?"

"I keep hoping." Christy quipped as she eased out of her beige, full-length, double-breasted coat.

"New coat?" Tucker asked as he threw his and Christy's wraps over his arm. He would carry them into the health education classroom across the hall.

"Mother and Daddy planned to give me the coat for Christmas," she said proudly. "They thought I'd enjoy wearing it this evening."

"It's nice." Tucker's eyebrows raised as he ran his fingers over the softness of the wool.

Just as Tucker finished removing Christy's coat, Vaughn Monroe's mellow voice sang out over the speaker attached to the record player.

Let it Snow,
Let it Snow,
Let it Snow, [1]

Monroe sang the smooth-as-silk words as white confetti fluttered to the hardwood floor.

Christy opened her hand and caught a few of the "flakes" on her finger. "Oh, what fun," she giggled.

"Well, if it isn't the youngest McBride," Morty sneered when Tucker walked by.

"And the fun melts from Morty's hot breath," Christy whispered lowly.

Tucker was determined to be polite. He knew the three untamed boys wouldn't cause any trouble there in the school. An invisible leash seemed to control them a little within the brick walls. "Hi, guys." Tucker acknowledged. Besides, Vinny seemed to be changing since he started going to church. Maybe he was turning into a normal kid. At least his sharp mouth had lost its edge.

Leaving footprints in the paper snowflakes, Tucker eased past Morty, nearly nose to nose, so close Tucker could smell the garlic on the boy's breath. Tucker met the kid eye to eye and didn't blink. Casually, he explained, "Just putting our coats away." He and Christy walked into the classroom assigned for all the coats. "I don't think the principal wants everyone to wander around the school and hang their coat in their locker."

Tucker took his time among the piles of outerwear. Smoothing the coats out he ignored the feeling of Morty hovering over his shoulder.

When Tucker turned, Morty was so close, that Tucker clomped down on his toe. "Oh, sorry," Tucker pretended an apology. "Am I in your way?"

Morty opened his mouth and squinted his eyes, but said nothing. As Mrs. Hunter brought her coat into the room, Morty only snorted.

"Good evening, boys." She smiled and turned to leave. "Have fun."

Tucker saw that Christy already left the room. But he still took his time, as one in charge of himself. He ambled out of the room and found Christy talking to Freddie Cooper and Anna Frederick near the punch table. Christy had poured a cup of the red fruity drink for herself and one for Tucker. He saw Freddie edging as close to Anna as he could. But it was Christy who looked different. Tucker couldn't take his eyes off her. Christy, his friend since they met in the toddler classroom at church, had changed. She looked like a young lady, not a tiny tot, and a pretty young lady at that.

Anna studied Christy's dress carefully. "Your dress is pretty," she admitted. "Mine got wrinkled minutes after I put it on," she whined. Anna was living up to her not-to-her-face nickname even at the Christmas dance … Miss Woe, with her frequent expressions of, "Woe is me."

Freddie wouldn't hear of it. "I don't see any wrinkles. Your dress is very pretty, Anna."

Anna blinked like she saw slim, red-haired Freddie Cooper for the first time. "Why, thank you, Fred."

Tucker, who was sipping from his cup, nearly choked. He tried not to spray red juice all over everyone's good clothes. "Fred?" Tucker gulped. Pulling his handkerchief from his pocket, he blotted his mouth.

"Well," Freddie stammered, embarrassed, "that's my name." He offered his hand to Anna as they joined the other dancers in the middle of the gym floor.

Tucker watched as the hardwood of the basketball court filled with friends doing the back step, triple step of the Swing dance. He shuddered at the thought of joining them.

Christy finished her punch and held the cup in the palm of her hand. "Freddie and Anna look like they know what they're doing."

"Um hum," Tucker agreed without appearing to be interested in dancing.

"Well," Christy announced as she took Tucker's cup out of his hand and placed both of them on a nearby tray. "We're at a dance. Are we going to whirl around a little, or not? If you won't dance with me, I saw Gilbert a minute ago. Maybe he'll dance."

"Wow," Tucker watched as Christy put the cups down, "you do have strong opinions about what a party should be."

"It seems to me, Tucker McBride," Christy insisted in a restrained scream, "if you go to a Bingo Party, you play Bingo. If you go to a Recipe Party, you eat and share Recipes. And, if you go to a Dance, you Dance."

"A Recipe Party?" Tucker grinned. "I never heard of that one. What recipes do they bring?"

Christy socked Tucker playfully in his arm. "Oh, come on, McBride." She grabbed his hand and pulled him to the edge of the other dancers. "We don't have to be in the middle of everything."

Together, they took a minute to study the feet of the other dancers, the ones who appeared to know how to dance. "It can't be that hard," he stammered as he struggled with where to place his feet. Tucker stepped once behind him, then took three side steps forward.

Christy grabbed Tucker's wrists and tried to repeat the steps. "You are doing it, Tucker. Now I have to live up to your progress."

In minutes, they were dancing the Swing, a dance that had been updated every few years since the days of the jitterbug. Tucker watched the other dancers add flips and swings to their routines and decided that fancy dance was not for him. Then, like any good athlete, he changed his mind and was soon able to enjoy the evening.

"And I thought it would be hard to get you to dance," Christy said with a tickle in her voice.

Tucker threw his head back with a laugh. "That's because I don't call it dancing. To me, it's physical exercise."

He kept his eye on the gruesome three. Vinny, Morty, and Gus didn't dance. Tucker watched them circle the crowd like they were wolves stalking their prey. After an evening of eating, watching the fun, and gawking at everyone, Tucker saw them slip out of the coat room with their coats and start to leave.

"How boring," Christy said as the three pushed each other out the door.

Tucker watched as the door closed behind Vinny and the other two. "They only watch life. They don't live it."

"I've got to rest a minute, Tucker," Christy gasped. "You've spun me around so many times on the dance floor, I'm dizzy."

Moving over to the few gym bleachers that were in place, they climbed a couple of steps and sat down. Tucker raised his eyebrows as he looked at his watch. "It's nearly eleven o'clock already."

Christy fanned her face with her hand. "We've danced all evening, ate tiny party sandwiches, and inhaled cupcakes. The only thing left to do is collect our Christmas present."

"Christmas present?" Tucker hadn't heard about a present or an exchange of gifts.

Christy looked toward the end of the basketball court. "The Student Counsel came up with the idea. Over by the basket keyhole, there is supposed to be a grab basket. There are fun presents inside."

Tucker studied the big red sack from a distance. "Let's go check it out before there's a stampede to the Santa bag."

Tucker and Christy watched the other dancers as they made their way to the free-throw line. Hurrying would have been awkward. Appearing to be two greedy kindergartners was not the picture Tucker wanted to project to his friends.

"Hi, Tucker ... Christy," Mrs. Hunter greeted when they got to Santa's bag. "Glad you two came."

Christy's eyes shined in the excitement and lights of the evening. "I wouldn't have missed it."

"I'm glad I came," Tucker admitted. "It's been fun."

Mrs. Hunter looked at the two and smiled. "The Council has topped off the night with a grab bag of gifts.

Small, fun things to enjoy. Just reach in and claim your gift."

Tucker stood back so Christy could reach for her prize first. He watched the excitement of pulling out a mystery gift. Christy's eyes widened as she drew out her hand with a small gift in her clutch.

The package was wrapped in red tissue paper with cellophane tape sealing the ends. "What do you think it is?" she asked Tucker. The excitement in her voice bubbled up all around her. The paper was removed and shoved into a waiting trash basket. "Look, Tucker … jackstones." Christy carefully pulled on the drawstrings of the cloth bag and dumped five small metal jacks with six tiny spikey arms, and a small red ball into her hand. "I haven't had a set of jacks for a long time," she said. Tucker could hear a childish excitement in her voice.

Tucker looked at the shiny jacks in Christy's hand and grinned sheepishly. "I challenge you to a game."

"You're on," Christy bragged as she put the pieces back in the bag. "You might be able to get a big ball into a basketball hoop ten feet off the ground, but jacks aren't about that. You have to be fast enough to grab one more jack with each bounce of the ball in order to earn the points you need to win."

"Right," Tucker agreed as he eyed the boys' grab bag and other students heading toward the prizes. The presents on the top felt soft within their wrappings. He didn't want to end up with a washcloth or a pair of long underwear. How embarrassed could a guy get? When his hand hit something hard, he pulled the present out and ripped off the paper.

"Tucker, a small wrench. You really like tools."

"Grandpop gets a new tool every month. He takes the bus into town to cash his pension check and then stops in Workinger's Hardware Store." Tucker rubbed the wrench on his trouser leg to make it shine. He held it closer, inspecting every inch. "I like it. It looks like many of Grandpop's. I can't think of anything better."

CHAPTER FIVE
An Odd Holiday Celebration

Tucker eyed the refreshment table as he and Christy started toward the door again to pick up their coats. The dimmed gymnasium was enhanced by small spotlights from each corner, doubling the light over the tables loaded with food. "Christy, a couple of molasses cookies and some punch for energy to walk home would be great." He stopped and selected several rich, spicy, dark brown molasses treats before pouring himself some red fruit punch. "I need the nourishment. I'll have to go a lot farther when I walk you home."

"Right," Christy agreed drolly. "Two or three blocks is a long way."

"It's a long way when it's cold outside," Tucker pretended to complain. "You better eat some walking fuel too. The food will warm our innards." He gulped down the fruity drink and smacked his lips. "Ahh."

Christy rolled her eyes. "Ice cold punch will warm us up?" Slowly picking up a cup of punch, she also selected a sparkling Christmas cookie with red icing and sprinkles. "This will probably turn my teeth red," she complained as she bit into the sugary treat and swooned over the sweetness.

Tucker sipped from his punch glass. "Oh … it should warm us by at least ten degrees." The sweet bite of cookie filled his mouth was spice and crumbly deliciousness.

Christy glanced at Tucker. "You win. I'll never have as many comebacks as you, Tucker." She put her cup to her lips and then pulled it away with a jerk. "This stuff smells funny."

"I didn't notice," Tucker sniffed at the punch. "I usually have a pretty good nose for food."

"How much did you drink?" Christy asked as she studied Tucker's punch cup.

Tucker tipped the cup up and peered in. "About half a glass I guess." As he brought it closer to his face, he smelled something … different. "What is in this?"

One of the last dances of the evening was to Al Jolson's music, "Toot, Toot, Tootsie." The entire room erupted into song. "Toot, toot tootsie, goodbye. Toot, toot, tootsie, don't cry. The choo-choo train that takes me, away from you, no words can tell how sad it makes me. Kiss me Tootsie, and then, do it over again." [1]

Christy sniffed her punch cup again. "Some kind of alcohol. Uncle Walter drinks alcohol. I recognize the nasty smell. Whenever we're over at his house, he drinks something, or several somethings while we're there. He gets very happy."

Tucker smiled. He remembered the legend of his mother's three brothers who got into the grape juice Gramma had canned for Communion at the church. The juice had been forgotten and left to ferment behind a whole case of green beans on a shelf in the basement. As the story goes, the grape juice brew was so strong, that it left the boys flopped and drunk on the cold cement floor.

Tucker looked up and down the refreshment table. "How did it get in the Christmas punch?" Then he glanced toward the nearest exit and nodded. "The three idiots."

"It has to be them." Christy stopped and stared at the invisible path to the door. "I saw the goofy triplets over by the table before they went in to pick up their coats. They were acting strange."

"Strange for them, or strange for the rest of us?" Tucker's left eyebrow raised.

"With those three …" Christy shrugged, "I don't think there's a category for them in a textbook of odd and strange behavior." She carefully placed her punch cup on the table. "I don't want even a drop on the red taffeta."

Tucker's smile was sheepish. "It is a very pretty, shiny dress." Then he snapped back to meet the immediate challenge. "Our coats," Tucker gasped low. "The threesome was in the coat room when no one was around." As he turned, he stopped at the next table where Mrs. Hunter was rearranging the remaining cookies. "Have someone dump the punch. It's spiked."

"Spiked?" Mrs. Hunter called after them. "How? When? Who?"

Tucker stopped and watched Mrs. Hunter ladle some punch into a cup. He nearly gagged when he saw her face screw up, indicating that Christy was right. Someone, probably the three fools, spiked the punch.

"We think it was Gus, Morty, and Vinny. Christy saw them messing around the refreshment table before they left. We didn't actually see them though."

"Morty had a funny flat-shaped bottle," Christy added.

"Maybe a flask," Mrs. Hunter mumbled as she brought a ladle of punch to her nose and sniffed. Shaking her head in disgust, she quickly checked the punch at the other end of the table. "This one is alright." She grabbed up the entire tainted punch bowl. "Tucker, will you help me carry this to the boys' bathroom? It's the closest place to dump it."

"Sure," Tucker agreed and wondered if Mrs. Hunter was going to go in. "I'll warn everyone inside you're coming in."

"Thanks," she said with a grin. "But when we get to the door, you're going to take the bowl in and pour the punch in the sink. We're closing up here shortly anyway."

With Tucker on one side of the heavy, leaded, cutglass bowl, and Mrs. Hunter on the other, they carefully made their way to the bathroom door. The red juice swished back and forth but stayed within the rim. Tucker turned his back to the door, pushed it open, and eased himself into the tiled space just as Gilbert threw a paper towel into the waste basket. The two boys were face to face over the swirling punch.

Anna Fredrick, following the punch bowl down the hall, stopped. She almost followed Tucker into the bathroom as she strained and gawked, trying to see what was happening. "Hey, where are you going with the punch?"

"This one is spoiled, Anna," Mrs. Hunter explained in a loose interpretation of the truth. "The punch bowl at the other end of the table was just filled. It's fine."

"Okay, I'll check," Anna added. "Thanks." Then she backed away quickly when she looked up and saw that she was halfway through the boys' bathroom door.

Tucker balanced the base of the punch bowl on the edge of one of the sinks and slowly poured the liquid into the drain. The bowl slipped a little, so Gilbert grabbed the glass.

"Here, let me help," he offered. "Do you want to tell me why we're pouring the punch down the drain?" As the two emptied the contents, the strange scent wafted up into Gilbert's face. "Booz?" he gasped.

"Yep." Tucker tipped the bowl up as far as it would go. "Get me some paper towel."

Gilbert pulled a few sheets from the dispenser and helped wipe off the rim just as Principal Metzger opened the door.

"Are you having any trouble with it?" Metzger asked as his hand remained on the door. "Mrs. Hunter said you were helping with a situation."

"Situation's over," Tucker said as he slipped a little on the wet floor tile.

"Watch out there, Tucker." The principal eyed the boy up and down. "I'll get Mr. Weaver to mop up the floor." He studied Tucker again. "Can you carry that heavy bowl, okay? The floor is quite wet."

"I'm fine." Tucker stepped carefully across the floor and took the bowl back out to Mrs. Hunter. "Where do you want me to put it?"

"Back on the refreshment table. We can take it out on one of the carts the parents will bring in to clean up everything in a few minutes." Mrs. Hunter patted Tucker on the back as he put the empty bowl back on the smorgasbord of sweets.

"Anything else?" Tucker searched up and down the full length of the fancy, red and green table. The entire length of the dessert buffet smelled like the peppermint sticks used for decoration. "Christy and I were about to get our coats."

Mrs. Hunter smiled. "I don't need a thing, thanks."

Tucker backed out of the gym as he surveyed the room. Christy took his arm to steady him. One more backward move and Tucker would run into the door jamb of the coat room.

Christy gasped while muffling a laugh at the same time. "Tucker McBride, are you drunk?"

"No," he denied emphatically. "I never drank alcohol in my life."

"Well … I think you did tonight." Christy grinned like she had just caught Tucker with his hand in his grandmother's cookie pan.

Tucker's eyes widened. "What if Gramma gets too close when I come in the house?"

Christy thought for a moment. "Put your hand over your mouth. Tell her they served garlic bread with cheese, and you know your breath doesn't smell very good."

"I can't lie to Gramma," Tucker blustered.

"You won't be lying," Christy protested. "I saw some breadsticks piled high with butter and garlic on the second refreshment table. You would just say that breadsticks were served. And your breath probably does smell bad … with alcohol."

"I don't know," Tucker stammered. When he turned to go into the Health Education classroom, he forgot about the punch bowl and focused on where he left his jacket and Christy's coat. The room looked like someone had come in with a cement mixer and agitated everything, then dumped it into a glob on the floor. "What in the…?"

"Oh, my goodness," Christy gasped. "Who did all of this?"

"I'll give you one guess with three names," Tucker growled, certain he was right. "Which three are the only ones who have already left?"

"Vinny, Gus, and Morty," Christy whispered through gritted teeth, her voice tight. "They better not have taken my new coat." She stomped toward the pile under which she suspected her coat was buried.

"And my jacket." Tucker began jerking coats off the floor. "Sam gave that deerskin to me. It's … special."

"There," Christy pointed to a beige coat stuffed under a student desk. Tucker watched her bend down to reach it. "It's so soft," she both admired and complained as it slipped through her fingers. With more might, she tugged on the sleeve like a pit bull.

"Christy, no!" Tucker warned. "You might tear your sleeve."

"You crawl under there and get the coat, Tucker. I'm mad and frustrated and ready to find those three and shove them under the desk."

"Since each has a head full of air, they should all fold up like envelopes, and fit under there," Tucker agreed as he freed the coat. Frantically, he searched under desks that smelled like erasers and last year's gym shoes. One desk must have concealed the remains of a half-eaten, three-day-old bologna sandwich. Finally, he spied the jacket and eased the leather from under the teacher's desk a few feet away.

Tucker and Christy walked out of the room, each wrestling with their own coat as they tried to straighten them and shake out the wrinkles. As they entered the gym, the voice of Bing Crosby was crooning the mellow song, "White Christmas." Tucker's eyes brightened as the music filled him with Holiday warmth.

Just as quickly, Tucker's focus on the great Christmas music faded into the background as something more practical gripped him. "Oh no," Tucker cringed when his coat was unruffled, and he searched through all of his pockets. "I left my billfold in my coat pocket because I was afraid that I'd lose it if we danced." Again, he pushed his hand down deep into each pocket. His shoulders drooped, and his face fell as the image of all his hard work at Butch's service station flashed before his eyes. He whispered in defeat, "The money for Gramma's Christmas present is gone."

CHAPTER SIX
Walking Home Can Be Curious

The moon squeezed through the overcast clouds as Tucker walked Christy home after the dance. A few stars twinkled in open spots in the sky above, but it was cold. Snow crunched under their feet. The homey smell of hickory wood from a neighbor's fireplace filled Tucker with the sweetness of an early winter bonfire. The closest Tucker could come to describing the aroma was when Maynerd's Meat Market smoked several hams and used hickory wood to create the fire. That scent filled his memory every time he ate a thick ham sandwich.

When Christy's fancy dress heels slid on a patch of ice, Tucker reached for her hand. "Here, Christy, hold on to me."

Christy snapped back, "I am perfectly capable of walking by myself. I'm not a toddler."

Tucker shrugged. "Of course, you aren't. I've never seen you toddle. And, a toddler wouldn't wear those shoes out on the streets in the winter."

Christy hit another frozen spot of black ice, grabbed Tucker's arm, and hung on tightly to his jacket, wadding it in her fist. "Well, okay," she agreed as she recovered from her near fall. "I'll hold on if it makes you feel better. You win."

"It isn't a contest," Tucker agreed. But smiling to himself, he envisioned a gold medal hanging around his neck. "It's not about who wins. It's about not picking you up off the pavement."

"I like that," she admitted. "The street is frozen and so am I. I definitely do not want to make angel silhouettes in the snow laying on my backside with bare legs."

Tucker walked a few steps in silence. "Sunday, I'll go to Chicago with Uncle David. Tim is flying in for Christmas."

"Oh?" Christy sounded surprised. "You hadn't said anything. How do you feel about Tim being home?"

"I can't wait. But I'll admit, I have no idea where he's going to sleep."

Christy spoke softly. "Tucker, it sounds like you'll be busy. Back at the school tonight, you also said your wallet was missing?"

Tucker's voice was low, and anger rose within him. "It sure is. And…all the money I earned for Gramma's Christmas present is gone with it."

"All of it?"

"Every dime," Tucker said flatly. "I carried it all in my billfold."

Christy tugged on Tucker's jacket sleeve. "What are you going to do?"

"Do?" Tucker stopped. "I know who took it. But how do I prove it?"

"Right," Christy agreed. "I can easily guess who stole it too. But I mean, what are you going to do about your grandmother's Christmas present?"

Tucker started walking slowly again. "We were making some nice things in shop class, but the school's locked now, and the projects are in there."

"Mr. Metzger lives next door to the school. He might open the building for you."

"Right. I got my assignment done, but a lot of guys still have some more work to do. I don't want to bother the principal. I'll call the teacher, Mr. Justine." For a minute, Tucker felt better. Maybe he could still give Gramma the class project he had been working on.

This school year, the first semester ended at Christmas break. But Mr. Justine gave the class the week following vacation to finish their assignments. The time extension was a result of the early blizzard that hit Elkhart County. School was closed for a week until the snow stopped and the streets were cleared. Mr. Justine was always fair.

The porch light at Christy's house shone through the icy air, creating crystal sparkles on the snow. Tucker could see Mr. Tree through the front window. He was sitting in his leather chair in his undershirt and pajama bottoms, reading the newspaper. Tucker could hear the faint sound of Christmas music coming from the family radio as Mr. Tree's head nodded in time to the beat. Christy's dad could be seen dozing off and then jerk himself awake. Finally, the man sat straight up when Gene Autry's voice sang out, "Here comes Santa Claus." With the volume turned up, Tucker could certainly hear most of that song.

"Thanks, for walking me home, Tucker," Christy whispered as she slowly let go of her grip on Tucker's sleeve. "And thanks for going to the Christmas dance. I wasn't sure you would remember."

"Sure, Christy. I remembered." Tucker ran the tip of his shoe through the snow that had gathered on the welcome mat at the front door. Before Christy could turn to go in, Tucker touched her shoulder. "I sure had a good time. I'm glad I went."

"Me too," Christy said and smiled.

Tucker waited until Christy was inside, then hopped down the porch steps.

He was filled with thoughts as he walked the three blocks home. He thought about calling Mr. Justine. *If he's out of town for the holidays, Grandpop knows the janitor's phone number. I think it's two long rings, one short, and then one long.* He trudged along the few blocks back to his house, making plans, and mumbling to himself. *If everybody else is gone for the holidays, I can stop by Principal Metzger's house.* It was settled. Tucker was determined to have a nice present for Gramma.

What? Tucker walked past the basement of the new parsonage being built across the side street from the church. He thought he heard a noise. At that hour of the evening, the cellar was completely dark. Peering into the open lower level with its freshly poured concrete walls and brick-faced fireplace on the south wall, Tucker searched the dark corners. *Wish I had a flashlight,* he whispered to himself. He bent over and pulled a pebble from the wet dirt and snow. With motions like Johnny Schmitz of the Chicago Cubs, he pitched the rock through a hole where the window would be installed. Listening intently, Tucker heard no scurrying feet, neither from an animal nor from a human. The eerie darkness smelled of damp cement. *Good thing the carpenters are going to add the first-level flooring tomorrow. They'd better get this thing sealed off before a family of opossums moves in.* He stood absolutely still, staring a few more minutes into the open basement. To Tucker, it felt like he was staring someone down, but no one was there.

• • •

As Tucker started walking again for home, he thought of Mr. Justine. Steven Justine was a great teacher. Tucker knew Mr. Justine would let him back in the school if he called him. But Mr. Justine was a new teacher at the middle school. He hadn't been there long enough for Tucker to know much about him. Tucker knew that Justine hadn't been from the neighborhood. Some people thought he may have grown up in the South because he still spoke with a small twang of a Southern accent. The teacher had talked a little about his family, his wife, and two sons, Jinx and Jason. But Tucker didn't know where Mr. Justine had been after he left the South, went to college at Indiana University on a basketball scholarship, and rented Mrs. Woodington's house a few miles from the school. Maybe Mr. Justine and his family weren't even home. Maybe they had gone south for the Christmas holiday, wherever home was.

Wait! Tucker stopped as he put one foot on the side porch steps. *Mr. Justine and his wife were chaperones at the dance tonight. I saw them over in the corner. He grabbed the brass doorknob and twisted. Unless they are leaving in the middle of the night, they're still here. I'll call him in the morning.*

CHAPTER SEVEN
A Movie with a Great Idea

Tucker was up early on Saturday morning, five days before Christmas. He jumped out of bed, knowing he had work to do. He was always busy. But today would be different. With his billfold gone along with all the cash he had tucked into the section for bills in the back, he'd have to earn more money. He not only had Gramma's Christmas present to buy, but he also had to replace his billfold.

The wallet was a gift from his grandparents the Christmas before. It was special in two ways. First, he liked the design in fine leather. It was slim, yet had plenty of space. Second, his grandparents gave it to him. Grandpop's pension was very small. The house on the corner had welcomed Tucker's mother and her older four siblings. Now, the McBride grandchildren were growing up there. A full house of love replaced the lack of money. They bought very few new things for themselves or the house. Whatever they already had, they took care of. Would the loss of his billfold be another opportunity for someone to criticize him for being irresponsible?

Tucker was not careless. He cared about everything. And his attention flew from one person or interesting situation faster than Joe could chase a rabbit out of the garden.

Downstairs, Tucker found his grandparents in the kitchen. Gramma was whispering to Grandpop. "Ja, ist gut Tucker went to the dance."

Grandpop sipped his coffee. "I just cannot see that boy dancing. Shooting a ball into a basket or wrestling his brother to the ground, yes. But dancing?"

"That would be quite a site," she laughed quietly and turned. "Tucker," she greeted when he walked into the kitchen.

"Good morning." Tucker heard what they were saying but chose not to pursue last evening's activities. Instead, he pulled a large bowl from the cabinet and the Wheaties box from the pantry.

Gramma tried to muffle a chuckle and asked, "Did you and Christy enjoy yourselves last night?"

"I was surprised. It was fun. And, the evening turned out to be very interesting."

"Ja?" Gramma's eyebrows shot up. "How interesting?"

Tucker thought for a minute. If his grandparents knew about the alcohol in the punch or his stolen billfold, he may not be allowed to go to another school activity. He never lied to them. "Well, Freddie and Anna surprised us with their dancing. They didn't do too bad. And Mrs. Hunter said she appreciated our help with some spoiled punch. We dumped it out for her." He thought a little more. "The gym looked nice, all decorated in Christmas ornaments and lights."

The clock on the wall gave him a way out of that conversation. He tipped up his cereal bowl, finished off his breakfast, washed and dried his bowl, and replaced it on the shelf. "Gotta run."

In recent weeks, Tucker went to work over at Butch's gas station on Saturday mornings. But since it was nearly Christmas, Butch gave Tucker most of the day off as a Christmas present. However, Butch's wife was having a family Christmas party that evening. So Butch asked Tucker to come to the station at four p.m. to work for two hours and close up the station at six. Tucker would be paid three times his regular hourly rate if he could help Butch out. Tucker usually didn't work beyond suppertime at five. No one interfered with Gramma's household routine if they could avoid it.

The last few Saturday mornings, Tucker helped dig the new parsonage basement but that part of the construction was all done. He smiled. George Garrett, the construction foreman, would be happy. One Saturday George thought Tucker was in the way, grabbed him by the seat of his pants and his belt, and tossed him out of the pit. "You're in the way, kid. Dig on the other side." With that, Tucker flew from the muddy dig and landed on his backside on the wet grass. His dog Joe licked his face in an attempt to soothe Tucker's humiliation.

The previous evening, while hanging around the refreshment table at the dance a little longer than most, Tucker, Christy, Anna, and Freddie made plans to go into Elkhart. The Elco Theater offered free movies on Saturdays to Elkhart County young people. That week it would be a Roy Rogers film, Tucker's favorite cowboy. He'd have to hurry. The bus would come about nine. The movie, *On the Old Spanish Trail*, started at ten.

All the usual characters would be in the movie: funny-man Pat Bradey, who was also the double bass player with the Sons of the Pioneers; Andy Devine and his squeaky voice as Constable Cookie Bullfincher; Roy Rogers, the singing cowboy; and Trigger, "the smartest horse in the world." The female actress and soprano singer, would be Jane Freeze as Candy Martin.

• • •

"I love this theater." Christy held onto Tucker's coat sleeve as she looked up at the 1400 lights in the dome ceiling above. "I love them both, this dome, and the crystal chandelier in the lobby." The dome had a thirty-five-foot span that stretched across the ceiling. Everything sparkled against the blue and cream walls and marble abutments that held up the arch of the stage.

"I like the colors," Anna said, looking up in awe. "I've been in here more times than I can remember, but I always have to take time to enjoy the ceiling."

Freddie went into the row first, followed by Anna, then Christy and Tucker. They all sat in rhythm.

Christy removed her coat and put it around her shoulders. "Whew," she exhaled. "We got here just in time." At that moment, the lights dimmed, and the audience hushed.

Two cartoons came on first. It was the second one that caused Tucker to bolt upright. Micky Mouse propped a ladder to the side of his house to retrieve the boomerang that had gotten caught on a lightning rod. Micky slid down the shingles on his backside and his pants started smoking but that wasn't what caught Tucker's attention. What caused Tucker's eyes to pop was the ladder that waited on the edge of the roof. When Micky hit the top rung, the whole ladder swung out until it teetered in a vertical position. Then Micky slipped down, knocking his chin on every rung he passed.

"That's it," Tucker gasped out loud.

Christy jabbed him in the rib. "Shh."

Tucker looked around to see if any of the guys from school were sitting nearby. He saw no one he knew but slumped down in the seat as far as he could.

When the title, *On the Old Spanish Trail,* spread across the screen, Tucker was still feeling giddy. He had a solution to Gramma's present. His problem was solved. But now, the cowboy with the white hat occupied his attention.

The movie unfolded with music and cowboys on horses. Roy Rogers helped out a group of his friends, The Sons of the Pioneers, who were unable to pay back the money they borrowed. There were wild robberies, a falsely accused gypsy named Ricco, and a beautiful young woman who completed the movie. Roy and his sidekick, Cookie, followed Ricco and discovered that Ricco was framed.

When the lights came back on, Tucker jumped up. "I have an idea." He checked his watch. "It's nearly noon. I'm not going to wait for the bus. I'm going to walk home."

"What?" Christy gasped. "You are not."

Freddie shook his head as a crooked smile crossed his face. "Tucker thinks he's the toughest, strongest cowboy in the saddle."

"Well, you don't have a horse or a saddle today." Christy glared at Tucker. "The bus will be here in five minutes. It's four miles back to Dunlap. It would take you over an hour to walk that far."

Tucker said no more but lined up for the bus when it arrived. He was excited. There was finally a way to get a Christmas gift for Gramma.

CHAPTER EIGHT

A New Deputy in the School

When Tucker got off the bus, he started walking north, not south to his home. "I want to make a stop first," he said over his shoulder as the frosty air from his breath circled his head. "I'll see ya later."

Christy shook her head at another Tucher detour. "I have to get home. Mom will have lunch on the table."

"Me too," Freddie said as he and Anna kept walking without looking back. Perhaps he recognized one of Tucker's *plans* starting to take shape and thought it best to eat lunch instead. Tucker's ideas didn't often end up as "planned." Maybe it was the way the corner of Tucker's mouth turned up in a scheming smile that gave him away.

The walk down the road gave Tucker time to work on the details. If the trap door was unlocked, it would be a cinch to get in. If not, he'd have to figure out something else.

The icy stones caused him to slip a little. He was glad he had worn his clodhoppers. The high-top shoes with thick soles protected his feet from the frozen ground. It was a cold day. The air was crisp and thin, letting the delicious barbeque aroma from Orvil Crumbaugh's backyard grill waft around to the road. Orvil enjoyed sizzling hamburgers. To Tucker, the scent of hickory chips smoking beneath the meat was like rugged aftershave Sam might wear. And, Orvil grilled almost every day. Unless a stiff storm came up and Orvil feared the burgers would fly away like they were snatched by a vulture, his grill was lit. As Tucker thought about it, he started getting hungry.

The parking lot of the middle school was empty. Light snow had fallen a half hour before, so if anyone had come and gone, their footprints were covered. Tucker slipped around the side of the building to the back where it faced the soccer field. A smile crossed his face as he put his hands in his pockets and pulled out his gloves. He wasn't positive he remembered to stuff them deep inside. They were the ones Gramma gave him for his birthday the month before, with leather palms and brown knit on the top. As he pulled them on, he studied the drainpipe that came down the corner of the building. With the agility of a ring-tailed monkey, he shimmied up the pipe on the wall, hand-over-hand, to the flat snow-covered roof.

Tucker knew where the trap door was. It led down into a janitor's closet in the hall opposite Mrs. Hunter's classroom. Goodness knows he sat on a stool in that closet often enough last year. Strange but true, Mrs. Hunter didn't always appreciate his sense of humor.

One day, while sitting in the dark janitor's closet, he looked up and spied a thin glimmer of light. Not an unadventurous boy, he felt for the ladder built into the wall that gave access to the shelves above. He had often used the wooden treads while helping Mr. Weaver put supplies away. On that one particular day of exile, Tucker climbed the ladder, hoping it led to what he imagined it would. And, it did.

Today, with Christmas just a few days away. Tucker had a real need to get inside the school. So, on the roof, Tucker used his shoe to brush away the snow from the opening. He could have found the trap door in his sleep, but it was nearly noon. With a great jerk, he tugged the square, wooden door covered in red roofing shingles. *I knew it*, he whispered to himself.

Tucker's plan would be perfect. He would get into the school from the roof, fetch his shop-class project, and be home by lunch. He quickly swung his feet into the roof opening, started down the ladder, and pulled the trap door closed. *Thank goodness*, he mumbled. He had to admit, it would have been more likely that the trap door was locked. *I guess Mr. Weaver forgot how much I like to climb ... anything.*

Tucker laughed quietly. *Maybe the trap door has been open since I unlatched it last year.* He smiled again as he counted the months in his head — thirteen. Then he cringed when the unlucky number occurred to him. Shaking his head to rid himself of the negative thought, he scrambled down the ladder and finally touched down on the floor of the closet. At least one foot hit the floor. His right foot sank into a ten-quart galvanized bucket Mr. Weaver used to hold mop water. His boot was caught, stuck tight. He couldn't shake it off. Each time he shook his foot, the metal handle clanged against the steel. He was not making the stealth entrance into the school building that he had planned. *A milk cow with a bell tied around its neck doesn't make this much noise.* He danced around the small closet, bumping into the shelves as the handle jangled like a burglar alarm.

There was no lock on the door. There was no need. What would someone want to steal out of Mr. Weaver's supply closet? It's not like no one would notice their theft. It would be hard to walk around the halls of the school with a five-foot broom handle in their hand without being seen. Besides, middle school kids rarely long to own janitorial equipment. Tucker opened the closet door a crack and peeked out. The hall was empty. Maybe the wide hallway would give a little more space to get the rattly-bang thing off his foot.

The hallway walls had that dreary, gag shade of institutional green before the fluorescent lights were flipped on. Then their shine had a strange bluish tint. Tucker had no plan to turn on the ceiling lights. Everything was silent. He would have had to clang down the hall with the bucket still attached to his foot. Exhaling slowly, he stayed in the middle of the hall and bent to set his foot free. Using a toilet plunger handle he had brought from the closet he wedged the wooden handle between the bucket and his boot and pried. He was so glad no one saw this production of a slapstick, self-cringing comedy.

With his foot free, Tucker started down the hall toward the shop class. Light from the windows Mr. Weaver had already cleaned during the holiday shutdown oozed into the hall as Tucker passed other classrooms. He slowed at each door, to make sure the rooms were empty. As Tucker approached the shop at the end of the hall, the sound from a whirling motor grew louder. Slowing, with a lump in his throat so large he felt like he'd swallowed an anvil, he stopped and peeked around the corner. A man in a heavy black coat, dark stocking cap covering auburn hair, and ear protectors was bent over the lathe on the north wall. Tucker had no idea where the courage came from, but he heard himself ask, "What are you doing in here?"

The man jumped as chips from the wood he was turning flew everywhere. He jerked around and cracked his head on the shelf above the machine as he straightened. "Oh," he moaned as he opened one eye. "Tucker?" He rubbed the back of his head, then looked around as if studying the room. "How did y'all get in here?"

Tucker smiled with a twinkle in his eye. "Santa and I have special ways." Tucker walked over to the lathe and ran his fingers over the maple wood. "It sure is smooth, Mr. Justine. What are you making during Christmas break?"

"Our little boys were tossing a football in the living room." Then his family tale speeded with frustration. "With as many times as Karen and I have told them both, it looks like they'd..." He stopped and shook his head. "Hank fell onto the coffee table and broke it. We're having company tomorrow. I'm turning a new table leg."

With the cracked, fluted piece of wood in one hand, Tucker compared the new turning with the leg the boys had crippled. "It's sweet, Mr. Justine."

"Thank you, Tucker. You're learning a lot about woodworking too."

"I have followed Grandpop to his workshop since I could walk," Tucker admitted with pride.

Justine chuckled. "It's Christmas vacation. I would think you would be glad to be out of here. And yet, here you are."

"I came to get my class project...if that's okay. Someone stole the money I earned for a special present for Gramma. So, I'd have no gift for her without the footstool."

"You can take it home, Tucker. I held them all here until after Christmas since many of the kids hadn't finished their projects. Y'all actually finished yours and I graded it this morning." He helped pull the workpiece from the corner, where it sat wedged behind Freddie's project. "You did a good job, I —"

"What are you two doing in here?" A man in a County Sheriff's uniform burst through the door, his hand on his revolver.

"Who are you?" Tucker knew Sheriff Springer and his deputy. The man ready to draw his gun was not either of them.

"I'm Deputy Fletcher," the man barked like a growling guard dog. "School's closed."

"I'm finished." Mr. Justine detached the new table leg from the lathe while keeping his eyes fixed on Fletcher. "I just have to put a finish on it."

"I said, the school's closed," Fletcher belched out again. "How did you two get in here?"

"I'm a teacher," Justine explained. "This is my classroom." He pulled the key out of his pocket and waved it in front of the deputy.

Tucker checked the identifying badges on the man's jacket. It said, Elkhart County Sheriff's Department. But who was this guy? "If you're a deputy, why don't we know you?"

"Beg pardon, kid. I don't know you either." He took
a step in Tucker's direction. "I asked, how did you get in
here?"

"I know everybody in the sheriff's department."
Tucker smiled. Maybe if he distracted the deputy, he
wouldn't have to explain that he had snuck into the
school through the roof. It could be, that the deputy
might not think Tucker was as cleaver as Tucker himself
thought he was.

The deputy didn't seem to find any of it humorous.
"A citizen reported he saw someone on the roof."

"Santa Claus?" Tucker laughed.

"That's it. You are trespassing," Fletcher insisted as
he put his hands on Tucker's shoulders, swung him
around, and slapped handcuffs on him. "Let's go."

"Wait a minute," Mr. Justine snapped.

"You want to be cuffed too?"

Justine glared at the deputy. "I'll call your cousin,
Tucker. He'll meet you at the station. Don't worry. I'll
run your project to my house then hurry right down to
talk to Sheriff Springer."

Out in the parking lot, Tucker was glad no one was
around to see him in handcuffs. If his grandmother found
out, she would be heartbroken. Stuffed in the back of the
deputy's car, Tucker slumped down in the seat so no one
could see him as they drove past his house on South
Main Street on the way to the sheriff's headquarters.

• • •

Inside the sheriff's office in the Court House in
Goshen, the deputy pointed to a bench against the wall.
"Sit yourself down." Fletcher unlocked the handcuffs
just as Sheriff Springer came out of his office.

"Hi, Tucker," Springer greeted with a smile and a hearty handshake. "How's your grandfather? Now you be sure to tell him I'll bring his spray paint can back this evening after my shift." He looked at Deputy Fletcher who still held the cuffs in his hand. "What's going on?"

"I found this muskrat in the school." Fletcher squared his shoulder like he was proud of bringing Tucker in. "I received word that someone was on the roof of the school."

"Yeah. It was probably Tucker." Springer turned and patted Tucker on the shoulder. "Were you on the roof again, son?"

"I sure was," he admitted proudly. "I left something at school."

"Was he alone in the building?" the sheriff asked the deputy, shaking his head at Tucker's antics.

Fletcher began to hesitate and stutter. "No, a teacher was there."

Tucker looked from the sheriff to the deputy. "Mr. Justine was using the laith in the shop."

The sheriff's eyes pierced through the deputy's badge. "Run Tucker back home, Fletcher. He'll miss his lunch."

The deputy opened his mouth as if to state a rebuttal.

"Fletcher," Sheriff Springer growled. "I can't have Rebecca Moyer mad at me."

• • •

The ride back to Dunlap was unusually quiet. But, since Tucker never met anyone he wasn't eager to talk to, he did drag a little information out of the sheriff's new deputy. His name was Dick Fletcher. His parents named him after Dick Tracy in the comic strip. Dick

Fletcher, not Tracy, graduated from Goshen High School and joined the Sheriff's Department when he got back from the war. He liked strawberry ice cream and played varsity basketball during his junior and senior years in high school. Tucker would have gotten more details if the trip was longer. But then, he knew he would be seeing Dick around … often.

The sheriff reminded him, "Stay off the school's roof, Tucker. It tends to make people nervous when they see someone walking around up there." He stopped a second then added, "I'd hate for your grandparents to hear of the shiny bracelets you tried on today."

CHAPTER NINE

It's Just Like Herding Sheep

At home, none of the conversations around the lunch table meandered off into questions about how Tucker felt in handcuffs. It seemed no one heard about the new deputy's first attempt at an official arrest. Tucker was certainly not the one to bring it up.

"How did the sheriff happen to bring you home?" Sam Treadway asked casually, like the sheriff often gave Tucker a ride.

Sam Treadway had been sleeping on the couch. The Moyer house had been full for many months. Sarah Harter had lived down the street from the Moyers after her husband died. Then, her dishonest landlord made it impossible for her to stay in her small apartment. So, Sarah had taken over Tim's room when he left for the Marines.

"It wasn't the sheriff," Tucker answered honestly with an edited amount of information. "It was the new deputy, Dick Fletcher. I got to know him a little."

"Where's he from?" Uncle Jacob asked. The other question, concerning how Tucker happened to get the ride, floated away.

"Goshen. He was in the Marines too." Tucker finished his soup and crackers. "Excuse me," he said as he stood up. "I need to run to Mr. Justine's house before I go over to the station."

"Why are you going to Mr. Justine's house?" His oldest sister Carolyn tried to help keep tabs on Tucker. There were frequent questions like: "Where are you going? Who is going too? When will you be home?" Actually, it took the entire neighborhood to keep an eye on Tucker McBride.

Tucker looked at his grandmother. Her head was down, scooping potato rivel soup onto her spoon. He put his finger to his lips and nodded in Gramma's direction, indication a need to discuss Gramma's gift. "The class left our projects at school, and Mr. Justine said he would bring mine home for me. He would have it at his house." He didn't add that his project was the only piece that Justine took home. That would only create more questions.

Tucker grabbed his jacket from the hall tree and darted out the door, slipping each arm into its sleeve as he went. The 1931 Model-A that Noah Dominick gave him, sat in the drive, its key was deep in Tucker's pocket. When you are fourteen years old, own a car, and drive it yourself, the key goes with you everywhere, even if the vehicle is parked at home.

Moyer Avenue, beside the house, ran back through the neighborhood and eventually out into the country. Tucker took that route to stay off Main Street. If Deputy Fletcher patrolled Route 33 between Elkhart and Goshen, Tucker didn't want the deputy to find him illegally driving.

Tucker slowed at the next corner where the church was building their new parsonage. He wanted to see how far George Garrett and the other volunteers had gotten with the floor joists, sealing in the basement while laying the supports for the first floor. A delivery truck from Lewis and Sons Lumber Company had just delivered the side wall studs when Tucker got there. Several of the men from the church were helping unload the shipment. Suddenly Tucker spotted movement. Was someone near the basement steps that were created when the concrete cellar floor was poured?

Well, well. What are we doing now? Tucker stopped and watched Gus and Morty sneak down the basement steps while keeping their eyes on the carpenters. *Vinny isn't along, so those two are up to more mischief than they can handle.* Tucker laid on his horn to warn Mr. Garrett.

Ahooga ... Ahooga. When Garrett looked toward the sound, Tucker made exaggerated hand signs pointing to the two ne'er-do-wells.

"Hey, you two!" George yelled, waving an impatient hand. "Get out of here or get to work." As he started toward the two, Garrett waved at the Model A. Everyone in the neighborhood knew it was Tucker in the old Ford. Looking back at the ruffians, Garrett started toward them. "Get!" He yelled like he was getting rid of invading polecats.

"It'll be an icy cold day in Palm Beach before those two go to work," Tucker mumbled.

Justine's family rented Mrs. Woodington's farm which was out on the edge of the country where the cornfields stood in stubble following the harvest. Mrs. Woodington's son, Archy, short for Archibald, farmed the land, not Mr. Justine. He farmed the forty-four acres along with his own one-hundred and ten. There was an adjacent sheep pen behind Justine's house.

Steven Justine's sons, Jinx and Jason, were out in front of the house, sledding down a small hill. There was still plenty of ice and snow on the little slope to make the Sears cardboard box their mom's new Kenmore sewing machine came in, slide pretty fast.

Tucker stopped the car and jumped out. The boys' speedy descent looked like fun. From the rumble seat he pulled a gunny sack Uncle Jacob used when he gathered black walnuts from the yard. Racing the boys to the top of the gradual slope, Tucker threw the coarsely woven burlap sack on the ground and dropped into position.

"Go," Jason ordered as all three propelled down the snow-covered hill.

Tiny ice chips spit onto Tucker's cheeks and mouth as they slid down toward the road. For security, Archy had stacked some straw bales along the foot of the property where the front yard met the road. His own three children came over for an afternoon of sledding with the boys from time to time. Safety was a necessity.

"We won!" Jinx yelled at Tucker. "You're bigger but we won!"

"That's because you're an expert sledder, Young Justine." Tucker laughed as he picked up his gunny sack. Grabbing the end of the box, he helped the boys pull it back to the corner of the side porch. "That was fun."

"Sure was," Jason agreed. Then he studied Tucker with one eye closed, blocking the sun. "Who are you?

"Tucker McBride," he answered in a tone that said, "Everyone knows me."

"Hi," Mr. Justine greeted as he came out of the side door from the kitchen. He held Tucker's class project in his hand. "I'll put it in the car." As he approached the

Model A, he looked around inside the Ford and then studied the hood, fenders, and doors. "Who drove you?"

Tucker flipped snow from the end of his clodhopper. "Oh, that."

"Dad!" Jason shrieked from the other side of the house. "They're out!"

"Oh no," their dad hollered back. He started running around to the back of the house, through the barnyard.

Tucker followed, not knowing what was happening. When he rounded the corner, fluffy, white lambs darted out of their pen and scattered in all directions in front of him. The boys were trying to grab the escapees as soon as they burst out of their confined space. It looked like they were trying to drive a mob of leaping kangaroos through a needle's eye. Tucker reached for two frightened woolies that bounded past him on his left, then spotted an amazing black one on his right. Reaching in both directions at the same time flipped him into a knot and dropped him in the path of three stampeding wool sweaters-on-legs. Landing on his backside, he splashed in a nasty puddle. Since the field grass was sparse, Mr. Justine supplemented the sheep's diet with a mix of barley and milo. The lumpy slush water Tucker found himself in was filled with melted snow, clumps of grains, dirt from the trampled ground under the gate, and a few droppings of Ewe Berries.

Jason squeezed two fingers over his nose. "Pee… yew."

Tucker laughed until he doubled over. The Justine men joined him in the hilarity, as he thought about the Slapstick Cop scene they just played. Even the lambs gathered around him as he sat in the bog. The black-wooly beauty crept up beside Tucker and sniffed his cheek.

"I'd say we've been herding sheep all wrong," Mr. Justine announced like any good instructor. "You're supposed to walk slowly, talk softly, and laugh quietly."

"Are you going to herd the kids in school the same way?" Tucker asked. He thought of Vinny, Gus, and Morty ... and decided that wouldn't work. There was no herding those three.

CHAPTER TEN

A Violin Merchant or Musical Muscle?

It was a long day, but Tucker paid no never mind. Every day was a busy one for him. And it wasn't over, not by a long way. After washing up and changing into clean clothes, he grabbed a handful of Gramma's best blackstrap molasses cookies, and shoved one in his mouth. Joe came up behind him and nuzzled his leg.

"Not this time, Joe," Tucker said as he raised the fistful of cookies over his head. "I've got to get to work."

Waiting until he got out on the front porch to brush the crumbs from his jacket, he flipped the tiny pieces everywhere and gobbled up the larger ones. Over his shoulder, he heard his grandmother call out, "Button up your coat and be careful on the street."

"Yes, Gramma." Across the street, he saw Butch Randolf pacing back and forth on the service drive. "Coming, Butch."

"I knew you'd be here, Tucker, but I was a little anxious."

"About going to a Christmas party with your family?" Tucker thought about his family and how much he enjoyed his half-brother's visit at Thanksgiving. For Tucker, family was the glue that held his life together.

"No, because I get a few hours off. The station has been getting some strange phone calls." Butch pulled his car keys from his pocket. "Now if you have any trouble, you call the sheriff. I'll not tolerate any horseplay at my business."

Tucker walked backward toward the station office to change his jacket. "Who is pranking the station?"

"Don't know." Butch opened his car door and looked back. "That Wagoner boy called and said to tell you that someone called —"

"Vinny Wagoner? Why did he call here?"

"He said, 'Tell Tucker, Lunchbox is back.' That seemed silly when he said it. I thought that Lunchbox might be the one making the annoying calls."

"Lundy Boxman? Yeah, I saw him in school. Some of the guys mock him and call him, Lunchbox. He's awkward, but pranking a business is a grade school trick. Lundy isn't immature. He just has a strange sense of humor."

"Well, whoever called, it doesn't matter now. You have a good evening." Butch started the car, pulled off the drive, and into traffic.

Just as Butch drove out, a fancy black car pulled up to the first pump. A man in a pecan-colored fedora hat stepped out and stretched. The smoke from his fat cigar circled his head and clung to his hat. To Tucker's taste, the weird scent of tobacco, mixed with the man's expensive aftershave cologne, was mildly putrid.

"I'll pump your gas for you, Mister, but you'll have to put that cigar out. Fire is dangerous here on the drive."

The man's eyes narrowed, and his face grew hard. Speaking low, he growled, "Young man, this cigar is a Havana."

Tucker gave him one of his friendly grins. "And it will be our brand-new Diamond T firetruck from Illinois that puts out the gasoline fire when your fancy Havana blows up this corner of Dunlap."

The self-identified gentleman didn't take his eyes from Tucker's. "Fill her up," he whispered with a glare. He didn't put his expensive cigar out, but backed away from the dripping gas pump and onto the grass that edged the highway.

"Where ya from?" Tucker asked in his usual friendly manner.

The fancy man snapped, "West of here."

"South Bend?"

The man puffed some more on his Cuban cigar. "Farther."

"Chicago?" Tucker asked, then stopped. He had heard rumors that Chicago Maffia bosses were going to meet in the fancy hotel at the lake. Then he remembered the phone calls. "Butch said you called earlier. Anything I can help you with?"

At that moment, a black 1939 Ford coupe pulled onto the drive. A boy in khaki pants and a leather bomber jacket jumped out on the passenger side. "Hi, Tucker. Dad wanted me to stop to get him a Coke."

Tucker spoke to the boy while keeping his eyes fixed on Mr. Fancy Pants. "Hi, Lun…Lundy. Great to see you. The pop is still over there," he laughed and pointed to the Coke machine beside the entrance to the office.

The man with the gangster-like voice admitted, "Yeah, I called a few times."

"Was Butch able to find what you needed?" Tucker asked. His mouth dropped open as he watched the man pull a small gold ashtray from his jacket pocket, snuff out the cigar, and put the unlit butt back in his mouth. He dumped the ashes on the drive.

The unlit cigar bounced up and down in the man's mouth. "Did the other guy tell you what I called about?"

Tucker looked at Lundy who was motioning frantically for him to come to the pop machine. "Are you having trouble, Lundy?" While replacing the hose on the pump, he shot a glance at the man again.

Cigar-man tipped up the end of the stogie. "I asked your boss if any Italians came through today with violin cases on the back seat of their car." He stared intently and smirked. "We have a little band."

Tucker couldn't help but crack, "A violin band? A few violins would be a small orchestra."

When Tucker put the gas cap back on, the customer pulled a twenty-dollar bill from his pocket and handed it to Tucker. "Keep the change."

"Thanks," Tucker gasped. "Twenty gallons times twenty-three cents a gallon costs four dollars and sixty cents. Your change would be, fifteen dollars and forty cents."

"Any violin-playing Italians come through here today?" the stranger in the double-breasted jacket asked again.

"I just got here a little while ago." Tucker felt his stomach flip. "Butch left as soon as I showed up."

At that moment, Freddie crossed the highway on his bike and rode onto the station's drive. "Do you still have any Payday candy bars left?"

"Ah, yeah, sure, Fred." Tucker looked at the man with a bulge on the left side of his fancy jacket. "Why don't you come back in a few minutes, and I can help you?"

"Come back?" Freddie belted out, completely unaware of the growing tension there on the corner of Moyer Avenue and the highway. "I'm here now. I'll just go in, take a candy bar, and leave five cents on the counter."

"Okay," Tucker heard his voice squeak out in a higher register. "Just stay in there and guard the cash register for me."

"Guard the cash register?" Freddie popped his bike stand and started inside. "You expecting the great filling station robbery?"

"Well," Tucker murmured, "there have been rumors."

As Freddie disappeared into the office, Lundy's long skinny legs bounded over to his dad in five steps. As he got to his family car, he reached in the window and handed his dad the coke.

Mr. Boxman leaned out and looked at Tucker. His face was ashen. As he tipped the bottle up, his hand trembled so much, small drops of coke dribbled on the shirt under his open jacket. His eyes widened and dilated, staring intently at Tucker. With a small tilt to his head, he nodded in the other man's direction.

"I told you to keep the change." Three-piece-suit-man pulled some dimes from his pocket and a small card. "If you see any Italian musicians like I described, call this number. It's on the back of my business card."

On the front was printed in slick letters:

Manny Bertelli

Stringed Instrument Wholesaler

Violins, Violas, Cellos, Double Bases

Michigan Avenue, Chicago, Illinois

Someone off-key? Hire one of our sweet instruments.

Tucker took the card and shuddered. Who is this guy? Why does he look so familiar?

Lundy turned and faced the station, rubbed his nose like it was running, and whispered. "He's a Chicago Mob boss. There was a story about him in *LOOP* magazine last summer."

To Tucker, it felt like his blood had stopped running in his veins. Lundy was right. He had read Uncle Jacob's magazine in July. Tucker tried to swallow the lump in his throat, but the baseball size sphere would not go down. He gulped again and called, "Hey, thank you, man."

"Prego," the man called out the window as he drove away.

"Tucker, you are thanking Chicago's biggest Maffia boss," Lundy warned in a gasping whisper.

Tucker swallowed hard again. "And, I'll bet, the rest of the Bertelli family went through our little town just minutes or hours ago."

Lundy threw his hand to his mouth. "Murder, kidnapping, racketeering —"

"Robbery," Tucker exhaled slowly. "Lundy, I wonder when the others actually drove through here? My billfold was stolen at the dance."

Lundy grabbed Tucker's shoulder and shook hard. "Robbers, Tucker, it might have been them."

Freddie came out of the building, chewing on a mouthful of chocolate and white nougat. "Robbers?" he questioned in a squawk. "Where?"

Tucker curled up his face. "Never mind, Freddie. Robbers? No Lundy. I didn't see any strangers at the dance."

"They're professionals," Lundy insisted, shaking Tucker's jacket until it started to slide off his shoulder. "He might come back," then he paused. "They might come back through here on their way back to Chicago."

"Are you boys all right?" Mr. Boxman asked with concern written all over his pinched face. "That guy was the real thing. That was Manny Bertelli, head of the Chicago mob."

Lundy's head nodded up and down feverishly. "Right. He's a drug dealer, killer, and thief."

"Who?" Freddie asked, bewildered.

Tucker smiled and took the business card from his pocket to show Mr. Boxman. "All of that, and an importer of fine violins. Or maybe just the cases."

Freddie shook his head. "Empty violin cases?"

Tucker put his hands in the posture of someone holding a Tommy gun like he had seen in some movies. His grandparents certainly did not have weapons in the house. "The *LOOP* magazine article said submachine guns are only thirty-two inches long. Those guns should fit very nicely in the viola cases."

CHAPTER ELEVEN
Get Ready, Get Set

Tucker was up early on Sunday morning, just four days before Christmas. He had his shop-class project stashed under a pile of old jeans and shirts in the attic and a gangster's strange tip in the back of his mind. Bertelli said that more of his so-called musical family would be coming through Dunlap. And, if you have a problem, one of their sweet "instruments" could be hired. Tucker shuddered as he thought about what those violin concertmasters would play.

He tried to shake off the memory of the steely gaze of the man who seemed to be offering friendship. He wondered if one of the company "instruments" would be able to find his billfold. An icy chill shot up his spine. He chose not to think about the total stranger who happened to pass through the area on his way to … somewhere.

Tucker would focus on the day in front of him. With his late hours after the dance on Friday, and a full day on Saturday, he normally would have slept another hour than he did that Sunday morning. After a busy day and a late night, even Grandpop stayed in bed a little longer than his usual rising at 4 am. If there had been a late gathering the night before, Grandpop might not come down for his morning coffee until 4:30. His years on the railroad created habits that Grandpop chose never to unlearn. But then, his morning ritual was developed over a lifetime. Grandpop started carrying water to the railroaders when he was only ten years old. He always said, "Long-established habits begin to seep into our bones and create the very frame in which we live."

"Mornin', Tucker," Grandpop greeted as Tucker walked into the kitchen.

"Morning, Grandpop." Tucker opened the cabinet for his favorite bowl and, by habit, the box of Wheaties. He dumped nearly half the box of wheat flakes into the bowl, added two rounded teaspoons full of sugar, and a lot of milk. He was careful so that the cream that rose to the top of the milk, did not slip into the bowl. Gramma saved the cream for Grandpop's coffee and additional baking.

"Looks like ya better pick up a few more boxes of that cereal you like, Tucker." His grandfather continued to look up from his steaming cup of java. "Ya daresn't run out. You'll be thinner than you are now." Grandpop's slight smile was enough.

"We can't have that," Tucker agreed as he squared his shoulder.

Grandpop looked at the clock hanging above the stove. "Your Uncle David will be here about a half past noon. As soon as he leaves the pulpit, he'll fetch his coat and come out here."

Tucker slurped up some more cereal. "It's Sunday. Gramma said she might do some quilting after her Bible study meeting. Grandpop, if you get out her quilting frame, I should be home in time to put it away."

"Thanks, Tucker," Grandpop said just as Gramma walked into the kitchen.

She pulled her apron from where it dangled from the refrigerator handle and tied the strings around her

Sunday dress of black rayon. During the war, all the silk was used exclusively for parachutes. After the war, when it was no longer rationed, a few church friends bought a yard of the fancy material for trim and shared some with Gramma. Later, when Gramma made the dress on her Singer treadle sewing machine, she made the collar out of the white silk that her friends gave her. "Ya, Tucker. I'm glad you're up. Your uncle will come soon after church. You'll need to lay out your clothes to go into Chicago with David to pick up your brother. Tim gets in at three o'clock, so you'll have to change quickly."

"Soon as I finish this cereal, I'll go up and lay out my Levi's and blue plaid shirt." He shoved another rounded soupspoon of cereal into his mouth. "When I get back from church, I can jump into my Levi's in a matter of minutes."

"Ja gut." Gramma checked her watch and the kitchen clock, just in case she forgot to fully wind the Gruen on her wrist. "The hymn book will be opened in forty-five minutes. Your cousin will start playing five minutes later. Tucker, finish your breakfast then start preparing for your trip."

Even though one of Gramma's granddaughters now played the organ for morning worship, Gramma had played the pump organ even before the new addition was added to the church. Recently, she had retired from playing every Sunday since the church purchased a new Hammond dual manual instrument. A few of the men carried the old pump organ across the street to the Moyer home. Gramma was only four-foot-ten and a half-inch tall. The new organ's pedalboard on the floor was too far from the bench for her to reach to play the additional notes with feet that fit a size five shoes. When she filled in for a sick or vacationing organist, she only played the two manuals above, like a double keyboard piano. Still, the schedule did not change regardless of who was playing the opening hymn of praise on the organ.

After Tucker took care of his bowl and spoon, he bounded up the stairs again to check out the clothes he planned to wear to Chicago. They were clean and pressed. Tucker had even used Gramma's iron to press a crease down the front of his jeans. He liked his clothes super neat and tidy. Hanging over the stairway banister, he shouted, "Gramma, I haven't worn my Levi's since they were washed. They are still clean. Can I wear them to church instead of my dress pants?"

The sound of feet slowly crossing the living room floor drifted up the stairs. "Well, now Tucker, that makes good sense. Ya, they are clean. Wearing them to church will save you some time afterward."

"You didn't say anything about lunch." Tucker took off his suit jacket and started to toss it over the stair railing in the hallway. Then he thought better of it and threw it over his arm.

Gramma's voice had a smile in it. "Your Uncle David said you will all stop in Gary, Indiana on the way home and have an early supper. You won't have time to eat lunch."

"That sounds great!" Except for mountains of candy bars, Tucker rarely got to eat away from home, unless you count the fiasco last year in Toledo, Ohio. But, never mind about that.

"Tucker." Betsy stopped as she came out of the bedroom at the end of the hall. "I like your casual look."

"Thanks." Tucker stepped back gentlemanly to let Betsy pass. His blue plaid flannel shirt puffed out as he tucked the back into his jeans. If his own sister thought school clothes looked good on Sunday morning, he knew he had found a new, relaxed look. Now, if Gramma would agree, he could put away his neckties.

• • •

The sanctuary of the church was alive with Christmas colors. Six evergreen wreaths with huge red satin bows hung from the walls, three on each side. A tree with white and gold Chrismons hanging on every branch was in the left, front corner of the room. Each beautiful Chrismon was lovingly cut and decorated by the Christian Women's Organization. The shapes were crosses, the Star of David, a chalice, the intertwining symbol of the Trinity, and so many more that Tucker lost track of the many sparkling designs. The scent of mint rose from the giant peppermint sticks that were gathered like bouquets and stood in walking-cane baskets up front near the piano. Tucker loved everything about Christmas.

The organist was playing "Oh Come, All Ye Faithful" as Tucker took his seat next to his grandfather. He loved to feel the melodic quiver through the back of the church pew when Grandpop's deep voice set the air around them vibrating.

The service was special for Tucker. He wondered which Christmas songs his mother had loved. Gramma said his mom was a good singer. Tucker liked that. He would close his eyes when the congregation sang, and imagine his mother was beside him, singing in harmony. The last hymn of the morning was "The First Nowell."

With the last note of *in Excelsis Deo* still hanging in the air, Tucker bolted from the second row.

"Hey, Tucker, where ya goin'?" Freddie stopped him in the hall. "Our Sunday school class is the other way."

Tucker turned to talk but kept on walking backward. "Tell Mrs. Kline I won't be there today."

"And why not?" Christy asked in a high voice, trying to sound like their short Sunday school teacher, Birdie Kline.

"We're going to Chicago to pick up Tim. Uncle David will be at the house soon. Gotta run." Tucker grabbed his coat from the rack in the hall, hurried out, and crossed the little side street to home. If Uncle David was going to get there before he had lunch, he would have to find something he could take along to eat so he wouldn't perish from hunger. Two slices of Gramma's homemade bread slathered thick with peanut butter and Gramma's luscious grape jelly, would fill up the corners of his stomach. The empty center of his belly would have to wait until they came back through Gary.

Tucker darted in through the side door and into the kitchen to create his culinary masterpiece. There was nothing better than Gramma's homemade white bread. Anything on top would make a perfect sandwich.

"Anybody home?" David Moyer called out as he followed Tucker through the side door.

"A whole bunch of us," Sam said as he hung his coat on the rack near the side door. "Here, Sarah, let me hang up yours too."

"Is there another cup of coffee around here anywhere?" David asked.

"Always," Gramma said as she sat on a dining room chair and removed her over-the-shoes, rabbit fur-trimmed galoshes. She pointed to the cups in the China cabinet. "We can always squeeze another cup out of the grounds for you, David."

"I should have brought a thermos of coffee with me before I left Elkhart. I am really tired," David admitted as he chugged down half of his mug of coffee. Replacing what he already drank, he explained, "A church member crashed his car about 11:30 last night. I met his family at the hospital and stayed with his wife and kids until he was stabilized."

"Oh, my gracious." Gramma patted David on the shoulder. "You are tired." She started for the pie safe. "Would a piece of pie wake you up or put you to sleep?"

"It doesn't matter, Mother. I'd love some of your pie." David stretched and scratched his head.

Gramma cut a piece of cherry pie and started to reach for a plate.

"Don't dirty a plate," David said with a laugh. He picked up the pie and ate it standing up over the sink where crumbs could be rinsed down the drain.

Tucker watched in awe. David took large bites and not a crumb escaped his lips. Joe stood patiently at Uncle David's heal, apparently hoping even a tiny piece would float down in his direction.

Holding a napkin under his chin, he wiped his mouth with one clean sweep. "Okay, Tucker, let's move out. We'll pick up your cousin Luke first, then … the road awaits."

With his P.B.J. sandwich in one hand and a fistful of Christmas cookies in the other, Tucker squeezed his jacket between his elbows and followed Uncle David out the door. Tim would be home for the Christmas holiday. Would the Marines have taught him some manners? Or, would Tim have learned to bark out even more commands, but this time, in double the time?

CHAPTER TWELVE
Chicago Adventures

Tucker had read many of Uncle Jacob's *National Geographic* magazines and knew about Chicago's Midway Airport. The great air facility had opened earlier in 1947 to meet the demand of those coming home from the war and the newly expanded businesses in America. Tucker was fascinated to read that Midway was named in honor of the Battle of Midway, a naval-air battle that raged over the North Pacific Ocean, between North America and Asia, during World War II. Tucker remembered reading about the Battle of Midway in one of Uncle Jacob's magazines.

There in the terminal, Tucker stood and watched through the large windows that faced the landing field. Flights were coming in fast, like a well-rehearsed square dance of do-si-do and allemande left. He remembered last July when Rex, a Dunlap friend, invited him to fly to a farm near Nappanee, Indiana. Flying above the stubbled corn and sleeping fields below was magical.

Even there at Midway, with the blue winter sky beyond the glass, the memory of his flight with Rex was as clear as if it were happening that day. As Tucker's mind drifted back to that moment in time, he remembered that Rex had landed on the Nappanee farm with a great swoop, and a bump, bump, bump across the grass. But it wasn't the landing that was a problem. The issue was taking to the sky again after Tucker and Rex fixed the rudder cable in another airplane the farmer had borrowed from Rex. Now, that was a problem! That day, not so long ago, when the sky bird reached a sixty-foot elevation, the right wing hit a tower that rose up near the barn and tore the wing away from the fuselage. The Cessna spun like a helicopter blade until it pancaked onto the ground. Tucker's forehead struck the instrument panel and immediately produced a welt.

Suddenly, Tucker found himself touching his brow and snapped back to the present. He was back in Chicago's Midway terminal where travelers raced in all directions. It was 3:02 p.m. when the Lockheed Constellation with its unique dolphin-shaped fuselage and triple-tail, put its wheels down and landed. Tucker remembered reading in *Popular Mechanics* magazine that Lockheed was powered by four huge engines. That day, it had flown all the way from Los Angeles, California.

Uncle David and Luke joined Tucker at the wall of windows to watch the incoming passengers. It was obvious that Luke's broken arm bothered him. He looked uncomfortable as he supported his right cast-covered arm by sticking his fist inside his buttoned-up coat.

The sky was a clear winter-blue. A woman in a black suit and a floppy red hat was the first one off the airplane. Her matching crimson gloves gripped the handrail as she stepped down and disembarked. Tucker took the man behind her to be her husband. He had his hand around the woman's waist. Gramma always said it wouldn't be proper for a man to hold on to a woman like that in public if he wasn't her husband.

One of the last to get off was Tim McBride. He looked grand in his green gabardine, belted field uniform jacket and matching pants. There were three stripes or chevrons, the military symbol for sergeant, on his upper sleeve. He wore a blue shirt under the jacket, a matching blue necktie, and a patrol cap.

Tim's flight from Los Angeles was long and crowded as others also tried to get home before Christmas. In his letter to Gramma, he said the military bus he planned to take to the airport would probably be full. All the guys were headed home.

Tim's basic training had been at Marine Corps Base Camp Lejeune in North Carolina. But Tim had completed his specialized training as well. Since he was good with motors, he was trained to maintain and repair tanks. While the war was over, the world still had restless spots that could break out into another conflict. One job of the military during and after WWII was to improve the Pershing and Sherman tanks. Grandpop said Tim was a man who could help with that.

Tucker watched as his brother hurried toward the terminal with his duffle bag in his hand. He was warmed when he saw Tim's face. His brother's broad smile seemed to say, he was excited about being home.

When Tim entered the airport terminal and saw Tucker, he stopped. "Tucker, you have grown! You're going to be taller than me."

"Timothy Arthur McBride," Uncle David called out as he slapped Tim on the back and gave him a side hug. "Tucker sure is. Your mama was short and I'm tall. Growing up, she was my younger sister and best friend, but she was sure little."

"I'm taller than Gramma," Tucker said with a chuckle. "But everyone is taller than Gramma."

"How was the flight?" Luke asked as a barrage of questions began to hit Tim.

"How high did you fly?" Tucker thought about his flights with Rex and shuddered.

Luke asked as he nearly jogged to keep up, "How long will you be home?"

"When do you have to be back?"

"Did you get airsick?"

"Are you tired?"

Uncle David yawned. "Well, I know I'm tired." When they got back to Uncle David's car, he stopped. "I'm too sleepy to take the wheel."

Luke backed away. "I can't drive with a broken arm."

Uncle David's eyes then shifted to Tim, as he studied him up and down. "I don't suppose you could drive, Sergeant. You probably haven't slept for a couple of days."

"I'd like to drive, but don't know if I'd remember how to maneuver in city traffic. And, besides, it's not a Sherman tank." Tim smiled at the Chevy Uncle David drove. "Besides, I would be asleep before we got out of the parking lot."

Uncle David squinted his eyes as he measured Tucker. "What do you think? Can you drive us home?"

"Sure." Tucker was excited. He drove his Model A all over Dunlap, but he rarely went out onto the highway. And the roads around Midway Airport were far more traffic-filled than two-lane country roads, or even Route 33 out in front of their house. "I'll drive us home if you just get me away from the traffic here at the airport?"

"I could. But Tucker, I think you can do it." David unlocked the driver's side door and walked around to the passenger side of the car. "It's only about an hour to Gary. You get us to food in Indiana, and I might be able to drive the rest of the way home." He opened the door and slid in. "But I won't promise."

Tim and Luke got in the back. In the rearview mirror, Tucker saw that Tim was nearly asleep before he even started the car.

"Okay, Buddy Boy." Uncle David reached out and patted Tucker's knee. "Just don't speed. I'd have a hard time explaining why a fourteen-year-old was driving my car."

"Aye, aye, Sir." Tucker put the key in the ignition and placed his left foot on the clutch and his right foot on the gas pedal. With both hands on the huge steering wheel, he started the four door, split-windshield Chevy.

The car sounded vastly different from his Model A. Rather than the higher pitched tin sounding put, put, put of the old Ford, Uncle David's Chevy almost hummed. The newer steering wheel may someday have that Bakelite smell like the A-Model Ford, but only passed the sniff test now when it was warm. The chemicals of phenol and formaldehyde gave the "first plastic" a unique perfume in the heat. Tucker knew it was certainly not warm that day. With his hands poised to start the trip, he looked out at a scene he hadn't expected. "It's starting to snow."

David closed his eyes and folded his arms in front of him. "The windshield wiper knob is there, in the middle of the dashboard."

Tucker hoped Uncle David would stay awake, at least until they got onto the highway heading east. Almost immediately, he heard David's heavy mouth breathing, followed by a rumbling snore.

• • •

Alone in a full car, Tucker had to entertain himself. In his usual way, drifting off to memories of fun times was his habit. Besides, he had to have someone to talk to. At least, his mental fantasies included friends and family. The pictures and people in his mind would be his companions, as soon as he got through the traffic around Midway.

As a fourteen-year-old, Tucker's city-driving experience was non-existent. There were no traffic lights on country roads around Dunlap. So, that Sunday afternoon in Chicago, Tucker had to be on high alert for a totally new way of taking to the road. He had no *driving memory* for city driving, where one drives like "usual." There was no "usual," or habit-driving, tucked away in the back of his head.

The traffic light at the first intersection past the air terminal changed to red as soon as he got there. A slight incline in the road at that crossing created a little foot dance. Tucker had to hold the car on the slope with the friction point of the clutch, while his right foot pressed the gas pedal. He either did the little two-step correctly or slid back down the incline. When the light changed, it was the clutch-accelerator *two-step* again.

When the light turned green, he pulled out into traffic. After leaving the drop-off drive and the surrounding roads of Midway Airport, Tucker turned south onto Highway 50. The snow started to blow in large clumps, creating intermittent gusts of blinding whiteouts.

At Oak Lawn, Tucker turned east onto US 20 and followed it all the way to Lake Michigan. The lake was bigger than Wawasee, a large lake not far from his Indiana home. Tucker smiled. The falling snow brought images of the many times he and his cousins and uncles had gone ice fishing. There in the car, with no one to talk to, the memory of the last time he fished through the ice was all that there was to entertain his mind.

The last time Tucker remembered Syracuse or Wawasee Lake having thick ice safe enough to drive on was during the previous winter. That was when Tim was still at home and the war had been over for a little more than a year. Rationing had ended, and even the limit placed on sugar had come to a halt in June of 1947. Still, Gramma had to carefully plan meals for a full house. Fishing was a way to put meat on the table. That particular fishing outing that occupied Tucker's thinking, Uncle Jerry had decided to drive his 1941 Willys American[10] a little farther out onto the lake's thick ice. Tucker thought Uncle Jerry's car looked like a giant, four-door, dark green marshmallow. In addition to Tucker and Luke, Uncle Jacob was along on that fishing trip.

On that clear and crisp day, the year before, all the fishermen on board the small car piled out. From the trunk, they pulled out the fishing equipment and four small folding stools. Then each one cut their own four-inch diameter hole in the ice using a special spear-like long-handled knife Uncle Jerry had invented. Just one of his many creations. Brushing any freshly fallen snow off their stool, they sat down and prepared to stay as long as it took to fill the family's frying pan. Nothing tasted better to Tucker than fresh fried fish that came from his own pole and line.

Sitting there staring at the fish line where it dangled below into the icy water was hard enough for an active boy. Tucker began to feel antsy all over. His nose itched, his leg cramped, and every muscle ached to move. The hardest was silence, especially because Tucker had read up on the topic. Sounds above the water don't really penetrate the surface tension of the water as everyone told him. And, the surface tension was frozen hard. So, there was no real need for him not to talk. Tucker suspected his uncles just wanted peace and quiet.

Tucker remembered, after hours of fishing, he had his usual zero-count of waiting perch. The fish caught by the other three anglers were lined up in a row on the surface of the ice. Then, suddenly his pole started bending. Just before they were to pack up and leave, something very large tugged on Tucker's line. He pulled and tugged until his line bowed into a derby hat frame. And still, the fish would not give up the freezing water below.

As the tug-of-war with the large fish powered on, Tucker leaned back into a mighty pull, hoping the scaley beast would fly out in time for him to take the huge perch home. At that moment, the power struggle changed. The perch poured on a counterattack and drug Tucker closer to the freezing water.

Smack. Tucker's backside hit the hard ice. There he sat as the freezing water splashed up from below. Luckily, the hole wasn't large enough for Tucker to be drug in, but his pants were soaked to the skin. As he relived the experience while driving the highways in eastern Illinois, he remembered thinking, *If I could just reach in and grab the fish.*

Just as suddenly, Tucker jerked his attention back into Uncle David's car. It was his job to drive Tim home safely from Chicago, but there was a growing problem. "I can't see," he whispered to himself.

The wet, icy cold wind off Lake Michigan brought in a fog that made visibility even harder. While following the curve of the road, the car started to skid and spin out. "Whee!" Tucker's excited eyes widened. An icy spinout to Tucker was like a ride on the county fair Tilt-A-Whirl.

As more spins seemed inevitable, he tried to remember. *What did Uncle Jacob say about spinouts?* He tried not to grip the steering wheel too tightly.

The car slipped to the left, then slid to the right, as a major skid took over his command of the car. With a controlled pull, he turned the wheel in the direction of the slide. The car slipped and swirled on the snow-covered ice. As he began to recover control of the big vehicle, he gently straightened the wheel.

Pumping the brake to slow the car, Tucker moved in behind a brand-new red, short cab Freightliner semi-truck. The broad big boy provided a wind break and snow shield for the Chevy. It felt to Tucker that he was hiding behind a big fry cook's broad apron. He followed the truck along US 20 as it eased southeast to East Chicago where he crossed into Gary, Indiana. Tucker wondered if it was snowing as hard in Dunlap as it was entering the western side of the state.

Tucker knew he had arrived in Gary when he smelled the foul odor of rotten eggs. They were passing the Gary Works, U.S. Steel's largest manufacturing plant, on the south shore of Lake Michigan. Despite Gary's unique perfume, it didn't dampen Tucker's appetite. His stomach began to knot, and he started watching for a restaurant. Nothing could interfere with Tucker's constant need for food. He was getting hungry. But then, he was always hungry.

Sounds from the backseat told him that Tim was rousing. Tucker didn't think that his brother had moved from his sprawled-out take-over of two-thirds of the seat position since he first fell asleep. Luke's space was crowded into the tiny space that was left, with Tim's elbow thrust in his direction.

"Uncle David," Tucker nudged on his uncle's arm, "Where did you want to eat? I don't know any of the places in this part of Indiana."

"Huh? What?" David opened his eyes and watched the heavy snow falling. "Has it been snowing this hard all the way? How did you drive in all this stuff?"

"Behind the semi." Tucker pointed. "I tailed that truck." He actually felt in control of his driving. It seemed to him he may have even saved Uncle David's car from piling into a snow drift or crashing into an oncoming car.

"Why didn't you wake me?" Uncle David didn't sound angry. He sounded sympathetic to Tucker's complete inexperience at winter driving.

"I'm starving," Luke yawned as he looked out on the blistering snow.

"You too?" Tim joined in. "I can't remember when I ate last."

With his pocket handkerchief, Uncle David wiped some of the fog from the windshield. "This looks bad, Tucker. Sorry you were initiated into the club of city drivers by tossing you out on an ice-skating rink."

"I skidded a little." Tucker kept his eyes on the road. "But it was fun."

"Fun?" Uncle David shook his head. "You make fun out of everything." He tried to look out through the snow and fog. "I planned for us to stop at Wilson's Bar-B-Q. It shouldn't be far once you get through the city. Wilson's is on the east side of Gary, where US 20 crosses Highway 12. It's not too much farther."

Tim scooted forward, crossed his arms, and leaned on the back of David's seat. He watched out the double panes of the windshield. "We had no highways like this in North Carolina. When will we stop? How much farther is it? I am hungry. I had a little snack-size meal on the airplane. But food ..." Tim drug out the food word, "I haven't eaten much since California."

Tucker knew that Tim was always a big eater. Around the dinner table at home, he had to watch out for Tim's flying fork. The three-pronged utensil might jab into the brown crusty fried chicken leg on Tucker's plate. And not so accidentally either.

"We're here," Tucker announced when he saw the neon sign glowing through the glistening snow. Careful to keep the car steady on the icy gravel, he pulled into the restaurant parking lot.

CHAPTER THIRTEEN
Another Chicago Businessman

Wilson's Bar-B-Q Restaurant was a long building parallel to the road. On the right side, green awnings arched the many windows like eyebrows on seven standing guards. A heavy growth of ivy climbed from the ground to the roof on the corner and between the two windows on the end. Tucker and the other three piled out of the car and nearly ran into the building. Their dash to the door was because they were famished, and food waited inside. But also, their haste was due to the drop in temperature, making their blood run as cold as the ice around them. It didn't help when a patch of snow from the roof fell on them when they got to the door.

Tucker and the family were seated near one of the large windows that faced the highway. "Bring the coffee." Uncle David pleaded with the waitress as she approached the table. He was still removing his coat and hanging it over the back of the chair when the waitress spoke.

"I'm Anna, and I'll be your waitress. What can I get for you?" An attractive young woman in a red-plaid dress and white apron poised a pencil over her order pad. "If you haven't been here before, we specialize in steaks, chicken dinners, and seafood."

"That's it." David Moyer looked at her name tag. "Anna, we will have four steak dinners, baked potatoes, green beans, salad, and pie, big whomping pieces of pie." He sat back, seemingly satisfied with his decision. "Sorry, guys. Does that sound good to you?"

"It sounds great." Tucker could already savor the juicy steak with honey Bar-B-Q sauce dripping from each bite. "It also sounds expensive."

"Now, don't you worry about that." David leaned toward the boys and lowered his voice to a whisper, so diners at other tables wouldn't be privy to their family's business. "Your Uncle Jacob chipped in some money. He knew it would take a lot of gasoline to drive up to Chicago and a kettle full of food to feed four large appetites on the way home."

Tucker smiled as his uncle whispered more about the origin of the expense money. How Jacob had earned more money over a longer period than he and not to forget his own bills with a wife and two children. Tucker remembered other visits Uncle David made to their house. His uncle and Gramma would stand in the kitchen and discuss simple family things. What to plant in the garden that year, or if the house needed fresh paint. But, even with all windows closed, they would still whisper.

Waitress Anna brought two steaming cups of coffee and two fountain glasses of root beer to the table. Each traveler sat back and sipped quietly.

"Well, we're inside, and out of the snow, Little Brother. After most of that snow landed on you, are you dry yet?" Tim asked Tucker. "Remember, I changed your diapers sometimes for Mama."

The thought of the Marine sitting beside him, changing any of his clothes, made Tucker uncomfortable. He had learned to be on his own without his big brother around telling him what and what not, to do. He cleared his throat and deepened his voice to an authoritative pitch. "The car's heater helped warm me up and readied me to dash in here."

In the parking lot beyond the window, a car pulled in, rumbling and belching. "Sounds like someone is having car trouble." Luke strained his neck and tried to see the entire row of cars.

BANG! POP! BANG!

Tim's eyes widened and his brow furrowed. It looked to Tucker like Tim stopped breathing, like time had stopped for him. Only muscle memory remained. Tim thrust his back against the chair. His hands nearly knocked over his coffee mug. Tim seemed to pull his head into his shoulders, like a turtle stalked by a predator. His face turned as white as a garden turnip. Tucker thought that there must have been something in his basic training or the workings of the Sherman tank that had left Tim frozen in a bad memory.

"Incoming," Tim screamed in a husky whisper.

Tucker's mouth dropped open. He had seen newsreels of major battles from World War Two at the movie theater before the major attraction started. But he had never experienced the effects of war right next to him at the dinner table. And Tim hadn't even been deployed. He had been in basic and advanced specialized training. But something had happened.

"No, Tim." Uncle David pated Tim's hand soothingly. "A car backfired. It's okay."

Tucker's expression fell. "Are you alright?"

For a moment, Tim covered his eyes with his hands. Then, without another word, he jumped to his feet and darted in the direction of the back corner of the restaurant. There was a sign on the wall — Men's Room.

"He'll be okay," David assured the others. "Mother said Tim was involved in a major accident at the base. They were all out practicing in a tank. Training rounds came in hard and fast. A recruit in the seat beside him was hit; he accidentally hit the gas pedal; and the tank hit a tree and shot down the side of an embankment. Tim was very heroic and helped get the others out of the tank. But he dislocated his shoulder in the process. He was taken to the hospital and they had him stay a few days. Not because of the dislocation. It was because of the loss of his friend. You don't forget those things very fast. It happened just a few weeks ago. I know we didn't get the whole story. But it was bad."

A man in a slick business suit sitting alone at the next table finished his meal and blotted his mouth on his napkin. As he stood, he placed a generous tip for the waitress on the table, then stopped beside Tucker. "War's tough, kid. But what I see of your friend, he's tougher. He'll be alright."

"He's my brother," Tucker corrected him. Suddenly, he felt overcome with a sense of pride. "And, my friend."

"You have a tough brother." The man pulled two dice from his pocket and rolled them around in his hand. "You people going to Chicago?" The fancy man asked.

"We just came from Chicago," David answered. "We're headed home to Elkhart."

"Oh yes, Elkhart." The man's smile was flat. "I'll be going through there on the way to the lake."

"The lake?" Tucker's voice caught in his throat. To him, it seemed like every wise guy in Chicago was headed for the lake to celebrate the Christmas holidays.

"Yeah. I'm meeting some of the family, some really good fellows." He tossed the dice up in the air a few inches and caught them again. "Did you see any guys driving through with ... a violin case on the back seat?"

Luke's eyes grew large. "Tucker, you were telling me —"

"Never mind, Luke." Tucker did not want to hear the word, Mafia. "I'll tell you more about that later."

The man smiled, revealing a gold right canine tooth as it sparkled in the restaurant's light. "When your young man comes back to the table, thank him for his service." The man brushed breadcrumbs from his silk, charcoal-colored, pen-striped, double-breasted jacket. The jacket had four buttons at the cuffs. He looked like a real dandy. But so was the man who stopped by the station the day before. In fact, they could belong to the same *fancy-man's club*.

"Your brother's toughness will return. I know my boys sometimes get ... tense ... after they've had their own type of war games." He stopped and slid his arm into the sleeve of his camel-colored topcoat. "Tell him I might have a job for him."

Tim came back to the table, patting his face dry with his handkerchief. "Sorry." His voice gave him away. Tucker could tell he was embarrassed. Then a sheepish grin spread across his face. "Guess I thought I was still in the tank." He nodded at the man but said nothing.

Tucker watched Tim and the Chicago dandy and wondered if Tim had any way of reading the man, of seeing the gangster beneath the suit. The "old Tim" would have sized him up fast. Tucker hadn't said anything, but inside he thought his brother was somehow different since he got off the airplane. Maybe it was nothing, but he seemed mellow, yet still had the same aggressive attitude as before. Tucker settled it. Tim was just tired.

"Never apologize, Marine," the man said sternly as he reached out for Tim's hand. "My a … company could use a fellow like you. Will you be out of the Service soon?" He patted Tim's shoulder.

The thought of Tim working for Mr. Big caused Tucker's stomach to roll. "He just finished boot camp." But the man ignored him.

"I think you'd fit in with my boys real good. You've had the best training. We'll get you a beautiful girlfriend. You'll see, your smile will come back. You can go a long way with a smile. You can go a lot farther with a smile and a gun." Mr. Fancy Pants said with a crooked smile.

Tucker knew he heard that last expression someplace. But, where? His friends at school didn't talk like that. He wondered about Vinny, Morty, and Gus. Then, he shuddered when he thought of the trouble Vinny would be in with his dad if he said anything like that.

"You can get farther with a kind word and a gun than you can with just a kind word."[2] He winked at Tucker. "I heard that someplace, kid." He artfully placed a light beige Fedora hat on his head, tipping it at an angle. "I've got to be going." He handed Tim a very familiar business card. Tucker could read it from where he sat.

Manny Bertelli Enterprises

Vincent Rossi - Associate

Stringed Instrument Wholesalers

Violins, Violas, Cellos, Double Bases

Michigan Avenue, Chicago, Illinois

Someone off-key? Hire one of our sweet instruments.

Tucker watched Tim study the man. "No, I'm not getting out yet," Tim insisted firmly. "I'm just home for a Christmas visit. There are a lot of us who can use a little break." He shook the man's hand. "But, thanks. I could use a job when I get out, though."

"Tim, no," Tucker blurted out. He jumped to his feet and took a deep breath. "The man said he lives in Chicago. Tim, the family would hate it if you moved out of the neighborhood."

Tim's eyes narrowed as he watched the man turn to leave the restaurant. Under his breath, he whispered, "Don't worry about it, Tucker." In Marine style, he didn't take his eyes off the Fedora hat. "I think I know who that guy is."

Tucker wondered how Tim could recognize a man they had all just met. Then, he tried to think of something that would be more attractive than big money from Mr. Big? "Ah, I know of a job. I heard the sheriff's department is looking for deputies in Elkhart County."

"They are?" Luke and Uncle David burst out in unison.

"Yes, yes, they are. Ah …" Tucker had to gather his thoughts fast. He wasn't really lying. Deputy Fletcher had just popped into his world. "I met a new deputy … yesterday. He said, ah … did I know someone else who might apply."

Tim shot a glance back at Tucker. "Why do they need so many deputies?"

Through the window, Tucker watched the "associate" as he pulled his coat more tightly around himself. He couldn't take his eyes off the man as he continued to watch Vincent Rossi, from his hatband to his mirror-polished shoes. The need for more deputies stood right in front of them, but it didn't seem smart for Tucker to say anything about that connection. Tucker just nodded when the fancy man saw him watching through the window, tipped his hat, and got into his Cadillac.

• • •

Tucker was glad they would be home soon. Gramma said she would have warm apple pie waiting when they got there. Tucker could always eat another piece of pie. Besides, with all the people in the house, Gramma cut her pies into small pieces. For a special treat, she had even sent Uncle Jacob into Elkhart for a fresh half-gallon of vanilla ice cream to go with the pie. The family churned homemade ice cream in the summer, but store-bought ice cream was a rare treat. Uncle Jacob brought some home occasionally.

The blinding snow near Lake Michigan followed them around the curve of the large Great Lake. With the lake-effect snow, their stop in Gary for Bar-B-Q, and Tucker's lack of winter driving experience, it was after seven p.m. when they finally got home. The lights in the living room glowed like a lighthouse beacon, welcoming them. The house on the corner in Dunlap was the home of David's youth and Tucker and Tim's home since their mother died. Of course, the side porch light burned brightly too. Gramma always left the light on when Tucker was still out. It made the half-acre seem warm and welcoming. He wondered if Tim was as happy to be home as he was.

CHAPTER FOURTEEN
But Everybody Knows

Monday was going to be a busy day. It was three days before Christmas, and Tucker still wondered if his school project would make the perfect present for Gramma. Now that he had picked it up from Mr. Justine's house, the old doubts of not being "shiny" or "perfect" enough haunted him like a ghost from the past. The snow that had thrown him left and right as he drove home from Chicago was still coming down. Besides trying to search for the Christmas gift, Tucker had promised Butch he would work at the station that afternoon.

When he was in grade school, his Christmas break was full of fun days with the guys. Freddie and Christy had already gone ice skating with the Youth Group from church on Sunday afternoon while he was in Illinois. Tucker missed out on all that fun. He had to admit, yesterday had been a mix of joy seeing Tim, the fun of driving, and the very uncomfortable, almost scary experience of meeting another Wise Guy, maybe from the old Marco Caruso gangster family.

Tucker had read in *Time* magazine how Frank Bruni took over Marco Caruso's gang after Caruso went to prison. Then in 1943, two other men were left in charge. Tucker thought all morning about the tough guys he met recently and wondered if they were somehow connected to the Chicago gang.

But he was fourteen. He'd have to set aside the Chicago Mafia. At that moment, he was doing the simple task of helping Gramma and Grandpop do the laundry.

"Okay, Gramma, do you want me to get more Oxydol? The laundry box looks like it's running low."

"Ya, Tucker. You'd better."

The washing machine agitated the clothes with the soap and hot water that Grandpop heated over the cookstove[6] in the summer house. "I'll crank the wringer, Gramma."

From the wash tub, Tucker ran the clothes through a wringer to get out most of the soapy water. Then he and Gramma transferred the clothes to the first rinse tub. Gramma rinsed the clothes by hand and tossed them into the second rinse water in the connecting tub. During the last step, Tucker turned the wringer around to face the last rinse tub, turned the crank on the mechanical wringer again, and squeezed the water from the clothes. Regardless of new schedules for the modern home one would see in Hollywood movies and women's magazines, in the house on the corner in Dunlap, it was Monday, and Monday was washday.

Tucker thought for a long minute about how he was going to ask the question he had to ask. "Do the Chicago gangsters ever come into Indiana?" Tucker didn't look up but continued to help Grandpop with the muscle work of washing. As Gramma prepared for the next load of laundry, they dipped ladles full of boiling water from the large brass kettle on the woodburning stove into the washing machine.

"Bertelli?" Grandpop bellowed. "Ya daresn't even think about men like that, Tucker."

"The Mafia?" Gramma gasped and stopped abruptly. "We'll not talk about gangsters."

"Right, Gramma." Tucker thought fast. "I just asked because I think one of the wise guys stopped at Butch's station the other day. I wouldn't want any of the younger cousins in the neighborhood to run into them."

"Oh, my goodness, no." Gramma ran some socks through the wringer and put them in the laundry basket.

Betsy had just come down the few steps into the summer house from the kitchen. "Gramma, do you want me to start fixing lunch?"

"Danke, Betsy." She checked the old clock hanging on the wall. "It is only eleven-thirty. We'll have the rest of the rivel soup I made yesterday. But before you start that, I would appreciate it if you would take this basket of clothes to the basement and hang them on the lines. Your grandpa's work pants would freeze stiff if you hung them outside."

"Sure," Betsy said as she picked up the heavy wicker basket full of wet clothes. Suddenly, she snapped back to the previous conversation. "Tucker, why were you talking about gangsters?"

Tucker stopped and looked from Grandpop to Gramma. "A fancy man came into the station on Saturday. And then, we saw another one yesterday in Gary when we pulled into Wilson's Bar-B-Q to eat. The man said he was headed this way. Both of those two guys talked about going to the lake and I ... I just wondered."

"Rumor has it—" Grandpop started but Gramma quickly stopped him.

"Let us not gossip, Pa."

"Well, now Ma, the boy asked. And it's not really gossip. We just don't know all the details."

Betsy put the laundry basket down again. "Everybody knows the Chicago gang spends time at the Golden Swan Hotel at the lake. It's on the other side of the lake from Uncle David and Aunt Karen's cottage."

"Betsy," Gramma gasped in a whispered voice. "How do you know such a thing?"

"Gramma, everybody knows it." Betsy picked up the laundry basket and started for the basement steps again. "They leave Chicago by train and get off in Nappanee. They're picked up there, and are taken to the lake."

Gramma looked at Grandpop. "Everybody knows?"

Grandpop's eyes were piercing. "Tucker, you saw one of those guys across the street?"

"Yes," Tucker nodded seriously. "He wasn't on the train. He was driving a fancy Cadillac."

"Tucker," Gramma warned, "don't pump gas for those people."

"Gramma," Tucker dabbled with the ladle in the hot pot of water, "I work there. I have to help whoever drives in. Besides, he said he was only a violin salesman."

Gramma closed her eyes and gulped. "Violins? Out of a Cadillac?"

"No." Tucker pulled the wrinkled business card from his pocket. "He gave me his card. It says his name is Manny Bertelli. Stringed Instrument Wholesalers: Violins, Violas, Cellos, and Double Bases. It says his store, or business, is on Michigan Avenue in Chicago. He added a little explanation. It says, *Someone off-key? Hire one of our sweet instruments.*"

Shaking her head, Gramma looked from Grandpop to Tucker. "You talk to everyone," she whispered lowly again as if someone were there listening. "Get the man his gas and whatever else he needs to buy, and send him on his way. The more you talk to him, the more he'll stay."

"Yes, Ma'am." Tucker knew she was right. But he loved to talk to anyone who happened to come his way. And, he had to work. He felt blessed that the station was just across the street from his home. He knew his billfold had been stolen, and he felt confident it was Vinny, Gus, or Morty who stole the wallet and his money. Now, he would have to work hard to earn it back. Tucker thought, *Maybe, all three of them did it. Perhaps all of Dunlap's gang of three participated in the theft.*

• • •

Gramma's rivel soup was fantastic as usual. Potato rivel was Tucker's favorite soup. He could have eaten three bowls full but one and a half bowls for each member of the family around the table was all the soup that was left. Carolyn was working at the telephone office and Uncle Jacob was at work. Sam had taken Sarah into town for something. Tucker didn't know what they were doing, but he knew their absence left more soup for him.

He scrapped the last onion piece and potato chunk from the bottom of the bowl, put his dishes in the sink, grabbed his coat, and headed to Butch's filling station.

"Glad you're here, Tucker," Butch called out from the bay. "I'll need you to run the drive. With all the snow, batteries need charging, fenders have to be unbent, and tires require patching from sliding into ditches not meant for driving. I've had some emergency calls to help those whose car won't start. I have had to say, 'Sorry, no.' Again, Tucker, thank goodness you're here."

"Why didn't you call me … or shout across the street?" Tucker said with a chuckle.

"You need time off too."

"Um, Butch, have any more Cadillacs come onto the drive? There was a really swell one here the other day. I don't see those very often."

"A Cadillac?" Butch hooked another battery to the charger. "Now wait. Yes, they didn't stop. But I did see a black one go by an hour or two ago."

"Wonder why so many have come through lately." Tucker hung his jacket on the hook in the office and changed into the jacket with the station logo on it.

"Probably another gathering of the wise guys," Butch said with a shrug.

"You know about that too?" He zipped up the jacket just as Mrs. Hunter pulled onto the drive. "You need gas again?"

"No," she said and jumped out of the car. "I need a map." She hurried past Tucker and into the office. "We're going to drive down to Nashville, Tennessee, the day after Christmas. Friends just moved there. We're planning our activities, like The Grand Ole Opry."

"Wow, that sounds great." Tucker loved to lay on the floor while Gramma listened to The Opry on the radio. Ernest Tubb was Tucker's favorite and Minnie Pearl was Gramma's.

"Nashville also has a quilt shop I want to find." Mrs. Hunter searched the rack of Sinclair maps for one of Tennessee. "I know there's a great store here, at the lake,

Coverlets and Quilts. They are probably the best and their prices are reasonable." She put the map in her pocket. "But I like to check out new places," she called back as she hurried to her car.

A bulb went off in Tucker's thinking. Butch would pay him for today, and he already received money for Saturday's work. But, would he have enough?

Everybody around Dunlap seemed to know several things. Everybody knew the Chicago mob used the Golden Swan Hotel as a place to "lay low" for a while, as some characters described in movies Tucker had seen.[3] And everybody in Dunlap knew that Tucker was a great guy but rarely finished what he started. Could that Christmas be when Tucker turns the car around and drives down a new road? Would he be able to complete the Christmas gift for Gramma?

CHAPTER FIFTEEN
A New Plan and A New Destination

It was Tuesday, just two days before Christmas. Tucker still didn't have that really special Christmas gift for Gramma. Since his billfold was missing, the chance to buy something else had been stolen away. He was able to get the class project out of the school, but he planned to give that to Gramma all along. There was no WOW quality to that Christmas gift.

"Tucker, will you please clear off the lunch dishes," Gramma asked as she started for her chair by the window. "I'm going to rest a few minutes. Goldie Washington and her choir from the African Methodist Church in town are coming out to practice for tomorrow's Christmas Eve Service."

"Mrs. Washington is coming?" Tucker grabbed up some of the dishes. "Is Johnny coming too?" He hadn't seen Goldie Washington's son for a couple of months. Both had been busy with their work, homework, and sports in two different schools.

"Goldie said he's coming along." Slowly, she sat down on the comfortable rocker and adjusted the pillow at her back. "After choir practice, Goldie is going to help me make, bake, ice, and decorate a large, fancy cake to serve to everyone after tomorrow's service."

"A Christmas Cake?" Tucker didn't want to discourage her plan but they usually had Christmas cookies after the Christmas Eve service.

"Pastor Daily said it would be a nice, special touch." Gramma closed her eyes. "He asked for a big one like a wedding cake only decorated in a Christmas theme."

Tucker thought that would be a really big job for Gramma. Lately, she had been getting tired easily. "Do you need me to stay and help you?" That wasn't how he planned to spend his afternoon, but he would if necessary. Then he added, "It's a good thing we're not on sugar rationing like during the war."

"The refreshment committee at the church paid for the ingredients. It's my turn to provide after-service refreshments. And Goldie said she would stay after practice and help me make it." Gramma pulled her sweater more tightly around her shoulders. "If you and Johnny want to go do something, go and enjoy."

Tim walked in looked round, seeming to seize up the situation. "Where are you going?" he asked. "I thought I'd use your car this afternoon."

"Tim," Grandpop interrupted, "that's Tucker's car. It's not yours to share."

"Thanks, Grandpop." Tucker finished clearing the table just as the doorbell rang. "I have an errand to run."

"When will you be back?" Tim pushed.

"No, Tim," Gramma joined in. "Jacob paid the car insurance for the Model A. It only covers Tucker."

Tim's fists doubled. "Tucker doesn't even have a driver's license."

"No," Grandpop stood strong. "Tucker has no license, and you have no car. Remember, you sold your car when you went into the Marines. Maybe one of your buddies can pick you up."

Tim glared, and then his face softened. "Sorry. One of the guys can stop by, sure."

When there was a knock on the door, Tucker opened it and greeted the visiting minister. "Pastor Gleason," he welcomed as he casually looked past the minister, searching for his friend Johnny Washington.

"Come in," Gramma said as she got up to invite in the pastor who was also the deep-base singer in the choir.

"Welcome, Pastor." Grandpop wiped his hand on his pants, then offered it in greeting. "Sorry. I was out in the workshop. A neighbor asked to borrow a tool."

"Goldie," Gramma called out as her friend walked in, followed by the entire twelve-member choir.

"Rebecca." Goldie reached out and gathered Tucker's little grandmother in her ample arms. "You're lookin' good, my friend."

Tucker checked out the window. "Is Johnny with you?"

"There you are, Tucker," Goldie laughed as she patted his cheeks. "Johnny will be here in a minute. He's taking the music over to the church."

"Gramma said I could find some activity this afternoon." Tucker collected his jacket. "Is it okay if Johnny goes with me? We'll be gone about three hours."

"Where are you going?" Gramma asked.

"Gramma, Christmas is the day after tomorrow. There are a few things we don't talk about at this time of year."

Sam followed Sarah into the house along with a gust of cold air. Each had broad smiles, but Sam's seemed to totally cover his face. "Christmas is full of surprises,

Becca," he said with a wink as he helped Sarah remove her coat.

Gramma looked at the two with her own small smile. "You two are grinning in harmony."

Sam helped Sarah put her coat on a hook. "I always find Tucker's plans ingenious, Becca."

"See you later," Tucker called out to anyone inside as he closed the door. He wasn't ready to talk about his new plan, so he kept going.

"Do you work this afternoon?" Christy asked as she came up the street, slipping a little on the packed snow at the side of the road.

"Hi, Christy. Glad you're here. No, I don't have to work, and I do have a plan."

Christy closed her eyes in a shudder. "Is it one of your risky plans, Tucker?"

"No … I don't think so." He draped his hand over Christy's shoulder. "Come on. Johnny Washington is in the church. You can use the phone there."

"Johnny? Oh great. I haven't seen him since Halloween." She stopped. "Use the telephone for what?"

"I'm going to go find Gramma's Christmas gift. I've made almost six dollars. Gas will cost less than fifty cents. Besides, Uncle Jacob filled the tank for me yesterday in case there's an emergency while he's at work."

"Where are we going?" Christy repeated.

Tucker opened the church door and let Christy enter. "Johnny's probably still in the Choir loft. He's setting out the music for the singers."

"Christmas Tree," Johnny shouted as he came into the hall.

"Johnny Washington, you are the only person on earth whom I allow to use my full name." She gave him a little hug. "Now, shorten it, please. Everyone calls me Christy, Christy Tree. Not, Christmas Tree, even though that's on my birth certificate." A little crooked smile crossed her face. "I won't call you John. That's my dad's name."

Tucker got lost in Christy's explanation. He had heard it many times before, and the Christmas present was the current focus of his attention. "Christy, if you want to go with us, call your mom and see if you can go to the lake. Mrs. Hunter gave me an idea."

"Which lake?" she asked as she started into the pastor's office. "How are we going to get there?"

Tucker shrugged. "I'll drive my Model A, of course."

Christy stopped in mid-step. "Three of us in your Model A coupe?"

He nodded matter-of-factly. "I haven't seen Freddie yet. He would have made four. That would have been a pinch."

Christy's mouth dropped. "Four of us in a one-seat car? I'll drive. The driver will be the only one with space to sit."

"You don't know how to drive," Tucker laughed.

"I'm a fast learner." Christy lifted the receiver from the phone's cradle. "Besides, Mom has let me drive around the school parking lot."

Tucker was glad Grandpop had just fought that same battle with Tim. "My car, my insurance, I'll drive."

She paused before she dialed the number. "I saw Freddie helping his dad cut that big limb off their tree.

The snow we've been having really weighed it down."
As she dialed, she asked again, "When will we be back?"

Tucker checked the clock on the hall wall. "We'll be gone about three hours."

Christy finished dialing. "It's ringing. Which lake?"

"Oh, right. There are a lot of lakes in northern Indiana," Tucker admitted. "Well, Mrs. Hunter wasn't talking about Lake Michigan. It's our favorite lake, Christy."

CHAPTER SIXTEEN

Snow Busting and Tiptoeing Away

Tucker had to admit, it was crowded with three of them on the bench seat of the coupe. He had seen other guys sit cattywampus to the steering wheel and decided to use their cool-dude approach to provide a little more space. He hunched himself at an angle against the window. That left a little more room for Christy to scoot over, so Johnny wouldn't have the door handle poking him in the ribs.

Christy crossed her arms and tucked her hands through the crook at her elbows. She looked like she was trying to roll herself into as small a ball as possible. "Tucker, you never did say what Christmas gift idea came your way."

Tucker's smile eased. "Mrs. Hunter came into the station. She was talking about places she and her family would stop at on their trip to Nashville."

"And—?"

Johnny asked the same question. "And … what gift idea did she give you?"

"Let's just get there first." Tucker wasn't ready to reveal the full idea. Everything he'd planned so far had either fallen through or had lost its Christmas sparkle. The money he earned was gone, and the school project had the taint of Deputy Fletcher's friendly treatment looming over it.

Once he drove out in the country around Goshen, avoiding major roads, Tucker relaxed. The sheriff's office was in Goshen. He wanted to leave a lot of space between himself and the shiny badges.

Tucker saw Johnny watch out the side window as snow-covered fields passed. "We go to the lake on the highway. I like your plan to stay away from traffic, Tucker. But it looks like there are fewer cars because these roads are barely passable with all the snow."

Christy leaned forward and glared through the windshield. "What are those people doing up there?"

Tucker slowed as the space between the Model A and the clowns in the vehicle ahead of them shortened. "They're snow-busting."

"Snow busting?" Christy put her hand on the dashboard and tried to lean closer. "With a farm tractor?"

Tucker could see that the tractor was slamming into fresh snow and then pushing it into the four-foot snow piles at the side of the road. "They mounted a snow-busting bumper on the front of the tractor. But why would they treat a new tractor like that? It can't be more than two years old."

"My uncle does something like that," Johnny said. "He actually gets paid to help shove the snow to the side of the road."

"Great, but I'm not risking my car. It might be safe. I know my A Model has a triplex shatterproof windshield, and the hydraulic shocks might help with the bounce. But we're not going to test it out to see if it works."

"Tucker McBride," Christy gasped in amazement, "did I hear you right? You aren't going to dive head-long into that snow? Where is the daredevil I've known all my life?"

"Well," Tucker teased, "if you really want to do some snow-busting."

"Never mind." Christy sat back. "I'll pass on that great opportunity."

Tucker had to swing the Model A wide around the snow buster as the tractor backed out of the high, icy drift. That was good for the snow-removing process but bad for Tucker. The path through the snow was narrow as the drifts gathered on both sides of the country road. Avoiding the tractor, his tires slipped and slid tossing them around on the icy snow. This is not how Tucker planned the day.

Thud!

The A Model busted into the bank on the south side of the road, tipping and teetering on the drift.

"No!" Christy shouted as if her command would keep the car squarely planted on all four wheels.

The Ford hadn't completely stopped but slid past the drift, and skated on the left door until it got almost to the farm lane a few feet east of the snow busters. There, it careened into the snow mounds. Tottering, the Model A landed half down on Tucker's side of the car. Then, it stopped.

"Everybody okay?" Tucker asked as he clung precariously to the steering wheel.

Christy landed on the floorboard in a heap, her boots flung unladylike in the air. Johnny slammed unexpectedly past Christy since she was now on the floor, and into Tucker. It looked like Johnny was doing his own version of snow-busting. All were scrambled like eggs in the skillet within seconds of the first slip on the ice.

Christy shook her head and sputtered. "Yes, I am fine, but not so comfortable."

Johnny grabbed the door handle, twisted it, and shoved it hard. "I think it'll open." It took a lot of muscle. At the angle at which the car had landed, he wasn't pushing out. He was pushing up on the heavy all-steel frame of the old Ford. He shoved hard, and the door finally popped open to the sky above. Fighting the weight of his own body, he grabbed the door frame and pulled himself out of the car through the trap door-like opening. "Come on, Christy. I'll help you."

Christy struggled with the force of gravity that tried to hold her body to the floor. Johnny pulled hard.

"I feel like I'm climbing out of a manhole." She positioned her feet safely on Tucker's leg and reached out into the snow that was beginning to gently fall again.

Tucker didn't think it was proper to push on Christy's backside. "How many manholes have you hauled yourself out of?" Tucker asked with a laugh. He decided it would be okay to help her in another way. He put his hand under Christy's snow boot, like an acrobatic act at the circus, lifted up, and eased her out of the topsy-turvy car.

Tucker's many years of climbing around in and on his family's home, swinging into the house through an open window, and reading comic books while resting in his hammock tied to the attic roof and the top of a tree, gave him all the experience he needed to slip up and out of the vehicle.

"Are you guys alright?" The tractor-driving man asked as he hurried over to Tucker and his friends.

"I think so," Tucker offered. Standing back and checking the car, he added, "I don't know if the car is okay." Though the tractor was the cause of his tipped car, and the reason for crawling out, it could be the solution too.

The man looked at the car and the way it teetered on the snow. "Sure is a nice old car. Does it belong to your dad?"

"No." Tucker patted the back fender like he was petting his dog, Joe. "It's mine."

"You're a young driver," the farmer checked Tucker over, along with the A Model.

"Pa," a younger fellow chimed in. "I've been driving since I was nine."

"That's a little different, Georgie. You drove the tractor all day during harvest when you were nine. But I never let you go out onto the road."

Tucker straightened as tall as he could until his chin stuck out farther than his nose. "I'm not nine," he boasted. "I'm fourteen. A friend gave me the car. I hope it hasn't been damaged."

"Well," the man pulled his gloves up, "let's get her up-righted and we'll see. By the way, I'm Luther Lehman."

"I'm Tucker McBride," he responded, his shoulders squared and tall.

"Any relation to Sean McBride?" Lehman asked.

Tucker hesitated. He hadn't heard the name, Luther Lehman, but he knew where he lived. They were all standing at the entrance to Lehman's farm lane. "Sean is my dad."

"Okay. Then you and your brother and sisters live with the Moyers, there in Dunlap."

"How do you know Gramma and Grandpop?" Tucker found it strange that he had not heard of Luther, yet the man knew all of them.

"Son," Luther laughed, "everyone in Elkhart County knows the Moyers in Dunlap. Most of your grandfather's neighbors have borrowed a tool at one time or another. And, the Moyers' friends are anyone who is friendly." He slapped Tucker on the shoulder. "Now, let's get your car out of the snow and right-side up."

Tucker, Johnny, and Christy got down in the ditch. Luther and Georgie took command of the two ends. "On three," Mr. Lehman instructed. "One, two, three." Hefting and groaning, the five lifted and pushed the old Ford until it sat on all four tires. "Now, can you maneuver the car away from the road's edge? It's all icy."

"Sure." While Tucker boasted he could get the car out of the drift on the icy berm, technically it was true. He had been in the car when Uncle Jacob had driven out of a snow drift. And, the winter before, Tim had described his encounter with deep snow and the steps he took to get himself out. But the truth of the matter was, Tucker had never driven himself out of the snow like he found himself stuck in that day. How could he have snow-driving experience? He'd only been driving for a few months, and that was on clear roads.

"You guys stay clear of the car, and I'll work it out of all this snow." Tucker pointed to a spot up the lane.

Christy looked at the snow piled under the wheels. "Why don't you just use Mr. Lehman's tractor to pull the car back on the road?"

Tucker was always amazed by Christy's logic. He wondered where it came from.

"That would be the easy way," Mr. Lehman agreed. "But your car is sideways to the road. If you can maneuver it around and still need help getting it out, the tractor can sure pull your Ford out."

Tucker quickly sized up the snowy predicament. "Christy, you and Johnny see if you can find some hefty twigs or branches." Tucker kept talking as he made his way to the back of the car, slipping and sliding around with every step. "Those gunny sacks I put in the rumble seat are sure coming in handy. They can be used for a whole lot more than Grandpop's black walnuts. When we gather nuts, we put them into the sacks before we take them in and dump them onto the scales at the hardware store."

Christy gathered an armful of twigs, and Johnny dragged a thick branch from under a tree in the side yard. Bringing them to Tucker, Johnny asked, "What is your plan?"

"I'll walk the car out. That's how Grandpop moves heavy equipment in the workshop or around the house."

Everyone watched as Tucker pulled a small e-tool, a foldable military entrenching shovel, from where he had stored it under the rumble seat. He knelt in the deep, freezing snow and dug the drift from under the wheels. "There, let's see if that works. Hope the car starts again."

Johnny took the shovel as Tucker got into the car. "If you need more snow removed, stay in the car and I'll shovel."

"I can dig out snow too," Christy offered. "I'm strong."

"I know you are," Tucker agreed. "In the third grade, you won every arm-wrestling contest anyone offered."

Tucker turned the key, put his right foot on the starter, and adjusted the choke. The A Model coughed and chugged, then leveled out in four-four time, to the music of the motor. "That's sweet," Tucker exhaled in relief.

Johnny stepped up like a private in the Army. "What can I do?"

Tucker handed the gunny sacks to him. "Here, put a couple sacks under the right rear tire. That's the drive wheel. The left one is just a floater."

Turning to Christy, he asked, "Will you put some of the branches and twigs under that right rear tire?"

"Will do, Commander," Christy giggled.

"Now, if the car will move, you'll have to replace sacks and wood as the car steps forward to help the Ford walk away from this drift."

Christy and Johnny put their assigned equipment in place and stepped back. Inching along, Tucker was able to coax the coupe a few inches forward. The two pit crew workers moved the sacks and sticks again, then waited. The tires gripped and slipped, then clenched the hard-packed surface of the gravely edge of the road. With a bounce and a jerk, the car lunged forward. The Lehman men cheered. Christy jumped up and down like a cheerleader, while Johnny twirled in a circle.

"You did it," Christy shouted.

Tucker stopped the car once he was firmly planted on the solid pavement of the street. "Thanks, Mr. Lehman. I'll tell Dad and Grandpop you helped us."

"Don't tell them that we crowded you off the road in the first place. I might have to use your granddad's shop equipment again in the future." Mr. Lehman laughed. "I'm joking, Tucker. But I would appreciate it if you would describe your afternoon a little different than what happened."

"I'll tell them that the roads were really icy." Tucker had no need to interfere with Mr. Lehman's use of Grandpop's workshop. Full of every kind of tool one could imagine, the small shop was a magical place for Tucker. Tucker would certainly protect Luther Lehman's welcome to Wonderland.

CHAPTER SEVENTEEN
Coverlets and Quilts

"Okay, McBride," Christy snapped teasingly, "we're at the lake. Did you come to the icy deep to Christmas shop for your grandmother? Perhaps she'd like a lake-front cottage."

"Of course," Tucker joined in the fun. "Two of them. One for Gramma and one for Grandpop, with an arched breezeway between the two."

"Right," Johnny laughed at the *Tucker-ism*. "Your grandpa won't even leave the porch light on for a minute longer than needed. I doubt he'd agree to buy a lake cottage."

Tucker looked down the next side street, then turned to the right. He smiled as he remembered one of Grandpop's favorite sayings. "Ya daresn't waste money on a store-bought cookie when your grandma always has a full cookie jar."

"My aunt has a shop down here," Johnny watched closely for the unique sign.

"I'm looking for *Coverlets and Quilts*," Tucker pointed to the corner in the next block. "There it is."

Johnny's mouth dropped. "*Coverlets and Quilts*?"

"Have you been there?" Tucker looked at the two empty parking spaces in front of the store. The snow was deep and packed hard. It looked like a layer of ice covered it all. He pulled as close to the curb as possible, in front of the quaint quilt store with colorful comforters hanging in the window.

"This is Aunt Jasmine's store." Johnny chattered on with excitement. "My mom brought a baby quilt down here to sell."

Tucker studied the two spaces and added. "Really? It sure is a nice-looking storefront." He checked the distance to the curb and added, "The edging on Gramma's quilt is torn. Her eyes aren't as good as they used to be. Small stitches are hard for her to see. I had enough money before my billfold was stolen. I have some money now but … we'll see."

"Someone stole your billfold?" Johnny shook his head as he helped Christy out of the car.

"Three someone-s," Christy added, then admitted. "I think I would have moved better with ice skates today." While Johnny gripped the door handle, Christy held on tightly to his hand and added, "We think it was Vinny, Gus, and Morty. Whoever it was, it was at school, at the Christmas dance."

Tucker held the quilt business door open for Christy. "Those three clowns were the last ones seen coming from the coat room."

Johnny charged in, waving, and hopping. Inside the store, Johnny called out, "Hi, Aunt Jasmine." He gave his aunt a bear hug.

"Johnny Washington? What are you doing here? Where's your mama?" Jasmine held him back at arms-length. "Let me look at ya."

"I came with friends." Johnny turned. "This is Tucker McBride."

"Ah, yes … Tucker McBride. Goldie told me about you." She put her hands on her hips and studied Tucker. "Young lady, that makes you, Christy Tree, right?"

"Yes, Ma'am." Christy's eyes popped at the same time as her mouth. "How did you know?"

"How do I know? Don't you realize your friend, Tucker, is renowned for his adventures, helpfulness, and mischief? Your last escapade landed you in Toledo, Ohio. How is today going so far?"

"Well …"

"We found out that Tucker is a great driver in icy weather," Johnny chimed in.

Jasmine gasped. "Did you have an accident?"

Christy waved off the bad news and announced the good. "He swerved to avoid hitting a snow-busting tractor. We landed in the ditch, but Tucker got us out."

"Well, good for you, Tucker," Jasmine encouraged.

Tucker changed the subject. "If you have a shovel, Ma'am, I'd be happy to clear off a couple of parking spots for you out front. More people will stop in if they aren't afraid of falling." He looked back outside as a car slowed then moved on.

"Well, now, that sounds like an excellent idea." Jasmine's eyes sparkled. "Before you leave, I'll bring the shovel from the back room. First, what brought you three to the lake? I know you're not here to go swimming."

"I came to see your store." Tucker looked around the cozy business with a wide smile. "I want to see if I can buy a quilt for Gramma for Christmas."

"For Rebecca Moyer?" Jasmine looked at the shelves of quilts around her. "But your grandmother hosts the quilting bee at your church every Thursday afternoon."

Tucker smiled to himself. "But Gramma would say, 'The quilts aren't made for me. They are sold and the money goes to our mission work.' That's how Gramma is."

"You look around. Then we'll talk." Jasmine winked at Johnny.

"There are so many," Tucker mumbled as he sorted through the stacks.

"And they're all so beautiful." Christy pulled out a quilt shaped like a rose. "I won't talk, Tucker. The quilt has to communicate with you, not me."

Johnny went to the back room for the shovel while Tucker searched the tables and shelves. "I'll get it started, Tucker. You shop."

Tucker unfolded quilt after quilt. It had to be the "right one."

"If you have another shovel, I'll go out and help Johnny," Christy offered.

"No," Jasmine said slowly, "but if you want to help, you can rearrange all the quilt squares on the back table. A lady came in a while ago and said she needed some squares for a crazy quilt. I think it will be more than crazy. She stirred the piles of all those patterns so many times, I think the quilt will be demented."

"Ms. Jasmine," Tucker said in awe, "look at this one."

"Isn't it beautiful?" She reached out and caressed the fabric. Jasmine obviously enjoyed the quilts she had in the store. "A sweet Amish lady brought it in. She hitched her horse to the big tree out front."

Tucker unfolded it a little more and spread it out on top of the display table holding more quilts. But there were none like this one. "It looks like the blossoms from the state tree, the tulip tree."

"Tucker," Christy whispered, "it is beautiful. I've never seen a quilt pattern like this."

"That's because it isn't a traditional pattern," Jasmine said with soft respect. "Mrs. Schwartz said her mother started making quilts after her stroke, as a therapy for her hands. Everyone in their family was gifted with one of her quilts, so she decided to start selling them. The yellow poplar is her favorite tree."

"How big is the quilt?" Tucker tried to size up the quilt by unfolding it completely.

"Here," Jasmine offered. Taking one corner of the hand-made work of art, she put it to her nose and stretched out her other arm to its full length. Then she replaced the length to her nose and threw her arm out again. "It will fit a very large bed."

"Wow, Ms. Jasmine. I thought Gramma was the only person who measured yard good like that. She said, from her nose to the end of her arm was equal to one yard." His eyes scanned every thread on the quilt. "I hate to ask, but I will." Tucker held his breath. "How much is it?"

"Sixty-five dollars," Jasmine said fast, then added slowly. "Mrs. Schwartz was in yesterday and asked me to mark it down 50%. That makes it, thirty-two fifty."

"Did you find anything?" Johnny asked as he came in carrying the shovel.

"Don't let that shovel drip in the store," Jasmine cautioned.

"I knocked off all the snow and ice, then dried it with my hankey." Johnny kept walking to the back room and placed the shovel beside the broom.

"He sure did," Christy sang out. "He did a great job."

Tucker knew the price was way beyond his means. He had six dollars in his pocket. The terrible trio stole over twenty-five dollars from him when they snatched his wallet. "It is great, but I only have about half of that. That is if I can get my billfold back."

"Well now, let's not give up too soon." Jasmine nodded toward Christy and Johnny. "Johnny and Christy helped me out a lot. I couldn't get anyone to come and shovel. Everybody around town needed a path cleared to their door and no one else was available. And, Christy, you helped a lot. My assistant had her third baby two days ago. I so appreciate your help. If you two would like to donate the money you earned helping me today, I'll add those three dollars making it about thirty-four. There would even be some change."

"But I don't have thirty-two fifty," Tucker reminded her. "Remember, the guys stole my wallet."

"I know. But, Tucker, you pray about it, and I think it will turn up. Take the quilt with you so you can wrap it up for Rebecca and have it under the tree. When you get your billfold back, give the money to Goldie and she'll get it to me."

Tucker never cried in front of others. That was certainly not his style. There in the store that day, he had to block the tears as he caressed the fabric of the quilt. That day would not be the day he blubbered like a baby and cried in public. But he knew that Christmas was going to be a very special one.

CHAPTER EIGHTEEN

The Lady in the Ditch Was Not a Lady

"Johnny," Tucker praised, "this looks great." The two parking spaces were not just shoveled. They were spotless, except for the continuing white flakes that fluttered to the pavement.

"Thank you," Johnny blushed. "I aim to do a good job."

Suddenly, a black car careened toward the Ford. "Watch out!" Christy shouted as she put her arms out to warn the boys to jump back.

The reason the big car swerved and landed stuck in the deep snow drift across from the quilt store was soon evident. A Lincoln Continental sped past Tucker, his friends, and the marooned black car. The driver never looked back. A woman from the stranded car, threw the door open, sputtering about the hit-and-run driver, hopped out, and waved her fist in the air.

"You just wait. When my husband catches up to you, you'll be sorry," she threatened.

Tucker hurried to help. "Are you alright?" Based on the woman's anger, he thought she had already answered his question. He put the quilt, wrapped in simple brown paper, and tied with string, in the car and laughed.

He turned to Christy. "It looks like you will either have to hold the quilt or sit on it."

"You bought a quilt?" the woman asked.

As Tucker focused his attention on the ditched car, he noticed it was a big black Cadillac. Suddenly, he stopped in the middle of the street as his stomach began to roll. "Yep," he answered casually, "It's a beauty."

The lady-of-the-car stepped gingerly through the snow. "What pattern did you decide on?"

"The edge has tulip tree blossoms," Tucker told her proudly, boasting a little about his wise purchase. She seemed safe enough, so Mr. Talker had to talk.

The woman extended her hand, "I'm Lana Bertelli."

Tucker gulped, "Any relation to Manny Bertelli?" He hoped she would say, "Who?" Or, "Never heard of him."

"Manny? How do you know him?" She looked from Tucker to the other two. "Manny is my husband."

Tucker saw Christy watching the conversation. He hadn't told her about his run-in with Bertelli at the service station. But Christy had a way of picking up on everything. When he swallowed hard, she noticed and immediately stepped back.

"I don't know him," Christy denied quickly.

"He stopped in where I work," Tucker explained to Mrs. Bertelli. He hoped he hadn't given away too much information. The lady looked nice, but her husband was like a character in a violent movie Gramma didn't want him to see.

"Oh," Mrs. Bertelli said with an "ah-ha" look, "there in Dunlap." She looked back at her car and shook her head. "He told me about a helpful young man. Now I'm going to have to go in the store and call him. He'll have to send some of the boys to get me out of the drift. He'll also want to know that One-Eyed Jack is the guy who forced me off the road. The husband will not be pleased.”

The thought of Manny Bertelli showing up with his “boys” to dig his wife out of the snow did not please Tucker either. A happy reunion to discuss One-Eyed Jack, whoever that was, was not the gathering Tucker was interested in. “No, Mrs. Bertelli. We’ll be happy to get you back on the road. We’re leaving, so you can re-park on this side. Johnny cleared it off real good.”

“Johnny?” she asked.

“Just Johnny,” he answered, uncomfortable with Tucker’s reaction to the woman. She didn’t need to know his last name. “Johnny John is fine.”

“Johnny John?” Her eyebrows shot up. “How interesting.”

“Come on, guys.” Tucker pointed to the Cadillac as he organized his pull-out plan.

Lana looked at Christy. “Are you one of the boys too?”

“Just one of the guys,” Christy said with a weak smile. It was obvious to Tucker that she didn’t want to get into a discussion with Lana Bertelli either.

Tucker got into the expensive sleek car and ran his fingers over the leather seats and the fancy dashboard. The keys were still in the car, so he tried the ignition. *Vroom, Vroom.* Through the open window, he shouted, “It turns over.”

“Okay, now what?” Christy pulled up her gloves and straightened her coat.

“I’ll keep my foot on the brake.” Tucker stretched as far out the window as he could to check behind him. “You guys get behind the car and we’ll rock it out.”

"How?" Christy's shoulders drooped as she stood haplessly behind the Cadillac.

Tucker shrugged. "It's like a while ago when we got the Model A out of the ditch after dodging the snow buster. We'll inch it out."

"I've helped my mom dig out." Johnny placed his hand on the back bumper of the car. "Christy, just do like I do."

"Push," Tucker shouted as he revved the engine. The heavy, four-door luxury car inched forward, then stopped. Tucker called out again, "Push."

Christy looked at Johnny. When the "Push" order was heard, they bent into the bumper and shoved.

The Cadillac's tires spun, then gripped a dry patch on the pavement and lurched forward. "Yeah," they all sang out.

"Oh, kids, thank you, thank you." Lana Bertelli threw her hands in the air and did a little wiggle dance Tucker had never seen before. "How much do I owe you?"

"We just wanted to help." Tucker turned off the engine, jumped out of the car, and handed her the keys.

"Well, I'll think of something." Lana grabbed the keys when Tucker tossed them to her, then shoved them into her pocket. She laughed. "I have three brothers. They were always throwing something around. I either caught it or got hit in the head with it, no matter what the 'it' was."

"Glad to help." Tucker opened the door of the old Model A and felt warmed. Gramma's gift was still on the seat. "We'd better go. I promised Gramma."

"Wait," Lana's voice tremored slightly. "I'm going to run in to pick up a special quilt I ordered, but … I'm a little afraid to drive back to the hotel by myself. If you three will accompany me, I'll have a friend bring you back to your car."

"A friend?" The old lump in Tucker's throat started growing again. Images of a crime movie preview, *The Gangster*, flooded his thoughts. A bloodthirsty gangster in Neptune City, Brooklyn, muscles in on a racketeer. A clash of the two "families" spills across the screen in violence. Tucker wanted no part of that type of "family" togetherness.

"Yeah." Lana's eyes sparkled. "Tucker, if you can help me just a little more, you can drive my Cadillac to the hotel if you want to."

"Oh, wow!" Tucker whispered. He beamed as all thoughts of safety floated away faster than they appeared. A choice for security flew away on the new mental image of sitting behind the wheel of the amazing Cadillac. "Sure!"

CHAPTER NINETEEN
The Hotel, the Piano Man, the French Doors

The Cadillac two-door Cabriolet – or convertible as some
called it – was everything Tucker could have imagined. He
had never gotten closer to an elegant car like that. He had just
drooled over them when leafing through the colorful
automobile advertisements in the magazines that came to the
house every month. For the winter, of course, the convertible
top on Lana's car was secured in place. But the thought of
riding along with the wind turning his hair into a jolly
scrambled mess didn't escape Tucker for a moment. He
opened the passenger side door and pulled the back of the
seat forward to let Christy and Johnny get into the luxurious
back seat. The whole car smelled like rich red leather.

After Lana Bertelli took the passenger seat, Tucker
ran around and seated himself on what seemed like a
throne. He paused in the driver's seat and ran his fingers
around the enormous steering wheel and across the
chrome-covered built-in radio. He caressed the shiny
gauges and the warm walnut wood trim.

Silence overtook the car as the motor hummed and
they pulled away from the curb. From the back seat,
Tucker could hear Christy and Johnny whispering. The
hushed tones didn't sound like fear. The conversation
was more out of respect for such a fine car.

"Crackers, Johnny," Christy whispered, "look at the
topstitching all around the leather seat cushions. My coat
doesn't have that much thread in the whole thing."

"Uh huh," Johnny breathed. "I don't think my shoes are even made of leather."

"Turn here," Lana directed. "The hotel is around on the other side of the lake."

"I know." Tucker turned the red translucent steering wheel to the left. "I've seen the Golden Swan Hotel from this side."

"You've never been in the hotel?" Lana turned and smiled at Christy in the back. "You either?"

"Inside the hotel?" Christy's eyebrows shot up. "No. Never."

Lana smiled and straightened in the seat. "Well, we'll just have to fix that."

• • •

The elegant hotel stretched out like open arms hugging the lake and welcoming guests. A large swimming pool and tennis courts were visible as Tucker turned the convertible onto the curved entry drive.

Tucker gawked at the massive doors with brass inlay and bevel-edged glass. A very stylish woman in a long fur coat entered the hotel. Tucker gasped, "It's even more swanky up close."

"Well, get out of the car you three. Let's go in," Lana said with a giggle.

Johnny got out but stopped and stared at the three-story building and whispered, "I don't think they'll let me just walk in the front door."

Lana tossed her head and set her jaw. "Why not? They'll do whatever I tell them to do. You are with me, Johnny John."

After Tucker and the others got out of the car, they froze solid in the place they stood. Standing in front of the hotel, it was more like a castle looming over them, than a public building where anyone could rent a room.

"I don't think I'm dressed for this." Christy pulled her coat more tightly around her.

"Nonsense," Lana said as she looped her arm through Christy's. "My dear, you are lovely."

Christy blushed and tried to clear her throat. "Thank you, Mrs. Bertelli."

The large front doors opened into the main-floor entry where a check-in desk and office sat on the left. When a man in wingtip shoes and a dark suit started down the grand staircase, Tucker shuddered. He couldn't see who it was but had no desire to see Lana's husband again. However, the chance to see the inside of the only luxury hotel he knew about was a once-in-a-lifetime opportunity. He felt torn between investigating every corner of the building, and running, like the fabled monster from the boggy deep had just surfaced.

The lake-floor level boasted the main gathering lounge, a large elegant dining room decorated in colors of cream and light blue, a bright sun porch, an expensive gift shop, a marble-top soda fountain, which was everyone's favorite, and some mysterious rooms with closed doors. Tucker nudged Christy and nodded at the enormous concert grand piano in the corner of the lounge. "Carolyn would love to make some music on that."

"I could get excited about playing that piano, myself," Johnny admitted with an embarrassed grin.

"Johnny," Tucker slowed down, "you play the piano?"

"Not in front of anyone." Johnny backed away from the large Steinway. "I'm no Scott Joplin."

"I heard some of his ragtime music on the radio," Christy added. "Can you imagine? His father was a slave. Then later, his son, Scott Joplin, played his ragtime music at the 1893 World's Fair."[7]

Tucker shook his head. "How do you know all of that, Christy?"

She shrugged, "Oh you know, you read here; you listen there." Turning to Johnny, she begged, "Please, Johnny, play 'Maple Leaf Rag.'"

Johnny opened his mouth to speak and paused. Then, he whispered, "Mom thinks I play like him. Joplin passed away a long time ago, but Mom says his music lives on in me."

Lana clasped her hands. "Sit down and play a little," she begged. "I would love to hear your music."

"On this piano?" Johnny gulped and desperately gazed around the large room as two patrons gathered for conversations. The beautiful room with blue leather chairs, glass-top end tables with brass lamps on top of each, hummed with friendly banter. But all Johnny could do was gasp. "In front of everybody?"

"What everybody?" Tucker said as he looked around. The man on the stairs had already passed and had walked on outside. Even the check-in manager was someplace in the back. Only the four of them remained, and the two strangers in the corner.

"Please play," Lana asked again.

"Well …" Johnny unbuttoned his coat and pulled the tufted leather piano stool away from the keyboard. Slowly sitting down, he silently ran his fingers over the keys. Then, like an explosion of excitement, energy, and Joplin-style ragtime, the musical notes of the legendary composer, Scott Joplin, burst from the soundboard. It was easy to see, Johhny was in a world of his own, bouncing along to the beat of the music. Gradually, a group of lake visitors who unexpectedly passed through the lobby began to gather around. Johnny didn't even seem to know they were there. He was startled when the last of the music was followed by a raucous applause.

Tucker threw his head back in excitement. "John, my man, that was great! You'll have to play that for Gramma. She might try ragtime herself. That'll keep Grandpop awake."

"Oh, my goodness," Johnny stammered. "I'd better leave. Mama will wonder why I've been gone so long." He jumped up and darted through the French doors to the right.

"Johnny, that's the wrong way," Tucker warned as he followed him.

They found themselves in the enclosed sun porch. Massive floor-to-ceiling windows were on two sides. The room was full of cream-wicker rocking chairs and a few tables with non-rocking chairs around the four sides of the table. Garden lamps hung from the ceiling. and a rock-faced fireplace covered one end of the room.

Christy looked around like she was in a daze. "Look at this," she whispered as she pointed to a seascape hanging on the wall. A boat with its sails windward beating against the wind skimmed across the sun-kissed water. "Mrs. Sanders, the art teacher, showed pictures of other paintings by this Indiana painter. He is really good."

Lana came in with a tall woman in a dark blue coat and sparkling crystal buttons. "Kids, this is my friend, Sondra." To her friend, she added, "These are the great kids I told you about, Tucker, Christy, and Johnny." She turned to the Dunlap bunch. "Sondra will take you back to your car when you're ready."

An attractive woman with red hair, in a specially made navy-blue pea coat, smiled back at them. "Hi, guys."

Tucker looked around the porch and then caught sight of another man's feet with expensive, black-and-white wing-tip shoes coming down the stairs. He was tossing two small objects in the air and catching them as they came down. "Hi, Sondra. Where is your car? We'd better leave." Tucker's eyes were not on Lana's friend, Sondra. They followed each step of the man in the fancy shoes, flipping dice.

Sondra pointed to the center window. "Actually, I'm right out there on the entry drive. We'll need to go back through the gathering room and lobby."

"We're in a bit of a hurry," Tucker tried to sound relaxed. Pointing to the center window, he added, "That window section is a French door. Maybe they don't use it often, but it is a door. Let's just go out this way."

Christy looked from Tucker to the French doors in that same old amazement. "Another *Tucker-ism*? We're leaving this beautiful hotel, through a window?"

"Well, now, Christy," he began and tried to causally nod in the direction of the approaching man, "it really is a door."

Christy caught Tucker's nod and nonchalantly turned to get a better look at whatever Tucker was calling to her attention. It wasn't a *whatever*, but a *whoever*. She quickly checked her watch. "Oh, my goodness. It's late. I have to get home." She casually inched in the direction of the French door. "It was nice meeting you, Mrs. Bertelli."

Lana seemed unaware of the growing concern between Tucker and his friends. "You too, Christy."

Before Tucker reached for the brass handle on the door, he turned back to Lana. "Are you all right now, Mrs. Bertelli?"

"I'm fine, Tucker." She gave him a little side hug. "After the car forced me off the road, I will admit, I felt really unsafe. I'm fine now. And, if you can wait a minute, I am sure my husband would like to thank you."

Tucker reached for the doorknob on the French door. "Well, our parents hadn't expected us to be gone this long. Gramma will get worried." He looked at Christy and Johnny and hoped they got his message about slipping out the door. "Tell Mr. Bertelli we are sorry we missed him today. And, we are glad to help you. Gramma is expecting me at home. And, believe me, nobody upsets Gramma … not even Mr. Bertelli."

CHAPTER TWENTY

There's a Lot to Learn and so Little Time to Learn It

On the other side of the French doors, the scene had changed. The snow had continued falling. It was much whiter than Tucker remembered when they went into the hotel. With his very first step along the cobblestone path, he slipped on the first flagstone his foot touched. Tucker waved his arms for balance like a multicolored whirligig[8]. He felt like he was part of the slapstick comedy act at the circus Uncle Jacob took Betsy and him to. But Tucker didn't want to be the clown that landed on the ground.

"Stay vertical," Christy coached anxiously from behind. Then, looking at the ice-covered stones, she added, "I don't think that hotel management intended for anyone to walk on this stone path."

Tucker wobbled as he regained his balance. "I think you're right. Since they canceled the 1944 Olympics because of the war, I have no ice skating stars to model my steps after. These Indiana flagstones are not the best way out of here, but it's the path I'm taking."

The snow had changed from the heavy flurries that came down before they went into Golden Swan, to clumps of giant flakes that clung to their eyelashes and hair. The heavy snow made each step slick under his feet.

When Tucker finally regained his balance, Christy grabbed the back of his coat and hung on. "Don't move too fast, McBride. I wouldn't want to pull your jacket off."

Tucker felt Christy wadding his jacket in a bunch. "Are you okay?" He turned back a little. "You too, Johnny. Are your feet still sole down?"

"So far," Johnny said with a chuckle. "Sole side down is the way I always wear my shoes."

Christy's teeth chattered. "I'm okay as long as you don't walk too fast. I'm shaking so much it may sound like I'm tap dancing rather than walking."

"Where's that Sondra lady?" Johnny asked as he looked behind them. "I thought we were going to ride back to your car with her."

Christy checked over her shoulder. "She said she had to get her galoshes. She'd be right out. She said we should go ahead and get into her car."

Tucker's teeth gritted a little to block a chatter. Finally, he took his last step on the slippery stones and stepped onto the plowed driveway. "I want to get out of here before Manny Bertelli catches up to us, so double-time it. I'm not interested in making a lasting friend out of Mr. Bertelli. Gramma would … no." Tucker stopped and smiled a knowing smile. "Gramma would introduce him to the Bible if he came to the house."

"Why are you so afraid of him?" Christy asked. "What's going on? How do you know Lana Bertelli? You seem anxious around her, and you're not anxious around anyone. And, Manny Bertelli? Where did you meet that guy? Who is he?"

"It's a long story." He searched the parking lot for a Sondra-type car - fancy, sporty, and expensive. "Look for a rich girl's car."

"I think I know who that Bertelli guy is, Christy," Johnny breathed out hoarsely. "I saw a big article in a magazine about Lana's husband. He's not a kindergarten teacher from Illinois. He's the mob boss, Manny Bertelli. Right, Tucker?"

"A gangster!" Christy gasped. "We've been hanging around with the wife of a mob boss?" She started frantically pacing back and forth. "Mother will ground me forever. She'll … what … ground me until I can't leave the house until my high school graduation? Maybe not even then."

"Shh," Tucker hushed. "Bertelli might be around here someplace. If not him, then one of his boys, his violin salesmen." Tucker jumped over another small pile of snow, slithering, and slipping. "Let's just get out of here."

Christy pointed to a plain, non-ritzy blue Dodge. "I remember, now. Sandra said her car was an old Dodge."

"That one?" Tucker stopped in his tracks in front of a 1940 Dodge, aged but presentable. "Uncle Jerry's car is fancier than that."

Christy squinted at the license plate. Around the edge was a special plate holder with a name inscribed on it. *Sondra Graham. Chairwomen: Lend a hand.* "I wonder what 'Lend a Hand' is. It sounds good. She might be okay."

"Let's check if the car's unlocked." Johnny darted toward the four-door sedan. "She told us to get in. I'm cold."

Johnny grabbed the handle of the back door of the well-worn Dodge, and Tucker opened the passenger side in the front. Tucker's shoulders relaxed in relief. "This is it. Thank goodness it's unlocked."

Tucker stepped back and jumped into the back seat. "Christy, you sit in the front with Sondra. Bertelli has never seen you. If he sees you through the front windshield, it won't matter. He won't put Butch's filling station in Dunlap together with the Golden Swan. I'll try not to look out the side window from the back seat."

All three settled into the car just as Sondra got in. "I'm glad you kids were able to get in the car. It's cold out there."

"It sure is," Tucker agreed. With no gloves, his hands had turned to icicles all the way to the bone. Rubbing them together to help bring the circulation back, he brought them to his mouth and blew his own warm breath into his fists.

Sondra unfastened the top button on her coat as she positioned herself comfortably on the seat "Lana asked me to take you back to your car. I am happy to. She said you really helped her today. Okay, where did you leave your car parked?"

Tucker scooted forward a little. "It's in front of a store here in town, *Coverlets and Quilts*. I bought a Christmas gift for my grandmother in there. It will be great, and a real surprise for her."

"Oh, that's one of my favorite stores. Good. I was just in there the other day." She started the engine, let the engine warm up a moment, and then began to pull out of the parking space. "There's Manny," she pointed to a man who was waving at them.

Tucker scooted down in the back seat until only his eyes could see out the windows. He didn't want to be seen, but he had to keep his eyes on Bertelli. There was a lizard quality to the man that made Tucker very uncomfortable. He didn't want that reptile to slither up to him.

"Do you want to stop and talk to him?" she asked as she waved back.

"No … not this time." Tucker yawned. "I'm awful tired." He closed his eyes then opened one a crack to keep his eye on Chicago's most notorious man of crime and philanthropy. A very strange mix to Tucker's thinking. "We really have to get home. We didn't plan to be gone this long."

"Sure." Sondra waved at Manny and rolled down the window. "Gotta run, Manny. Next time." She closed the window and pulled out onto the street.

Tucker watched as Bertelli waved again. With a short nod and wiggle of his fingers, he hoped a little wave would satisfy Bertelli. Tucker didn't plan on a "next time" and hoped that would be his last encounter with the stringed instrument salesman of Michigan Avenue. When Lana joined her husband just outside the front door, Manny put his arm around her waist as they turned and walked back inside.

Christy removed her gloves, opened her coat at the neck, and tried to appear casual. With Sondra's kind and friendly manner, she finally asked Sondra the question they all wondered. "Sondra, how did you and Lana meet?"

"We met in the first grade and were in the same Red Robbins girl's group together." Sondra turned the car to the left and headed into the village. "Lana and I also went to the same church and attended youth group together each Sunday evening. Pastor Ron and his wife, Joyce, were great. There were a lot of us in the group, and we were all close friends. When I was a freshman in high school, Manny was in the group, too, but he was a few years older. He didn't attend our church, just youth. So, we all thought he just wanted to be near Lana. They would sit together during devotions and Bible study."

Tucker couldn't see Sondra's expression. But he recognized her warm memories as she seemed to chuckle under her breath.

"Lana would ride in his car if we car-poled to go someplace," Sondra told them. "They weren't alone. Two or three of us would ride with him too. But it was Lana who sat in the front seat beside him."

Christy looked over her shoulder at Tucker. He had been listening to every word.

Tucker shrugged and shook his head a little. Who would have thought that Lana and Manny Bertelli would have been raised in the church? What on earth happened to him? At home, Gramma had coaxed Vinney to come to church. He seemed to be changing for the better. Would Vinny sink back into a larger world of crime once he was grown? Tucker guessed that would have to be up to Vinney. And Lana, she still seemed like a nice lady. Didn't she know how her husband made his living?

Tucker wondered if he would ever figure people out, especially Manny Bertelli. But then, maybe Gramma was right. She always said, "Never use logic to try to understand someone or something that's illogical. You'll exhaust yourself and waste your time." Gramma was right about everything else. Tucker guessed Gramma was right about people too.

Once they got back to the quilt shop, Tucker, Christy, and Johnny said their goodbyes to Sondra Graham. Tucker reached out his hand to her. "Thanks, Sondra. I'm glad we didn't have to walk back here from the other side of the lake."

Christy jumped in. "It didn't look like we were even able to walk around in the parking lot. It is really slick out here."

"I am very glad to help you all," Sondra said softly. "Tucker, Lana is the one who thanks you a million times over. That was the second time she was forced off the road. She is so thankful you were there to help dig her out."

Tucker blushed a little. "We all got her out of the ditch."

"Well," Sondra agreed but would not let him refuse a well-meant thank you, "Lana told me, you three saved her life."

"Wow," Johnny gulped, "I would have been properly scared if I had known that."

Tucker thought for a minute, then added slowly, "I think she should be worried about being forced off the road. If that was the second time, it was no coincidence. Maybe her husband has a rival violin company that would like to take over his customers."

Sondra nodded. "I never heard anything about that. But Manny has been talking about Lana not going out without a driver. She is so independent. She wants to jump in the car on a whim and go wherever her new idea sends her."

"Well, maybe you can talk to her about staying safe," Christy offered as she opened the door. "Help her learn to keep her eyes open."

"I will, Christy," Sondra agreed.

Tucker stepped out of the car and then leaned back in. "If nothing else, tell her to keep a notepad and pencil in the car so she can write down the other car's license number if someone gets too close. She would have real evidence to give to the police." Even as he spoke, Tucker wondered if Bertelli would involve the police in anything.

"You all are such a blessing." Sondra smiled and pulled back into traffic.

"Come on, guys, let's go." Tucker opened the car door to the A Model and studied the large wrapped quilt in the middle of the seat. "I'm glad I closed the windows. The gift could have collected snow."

"Where are we going to sit?" Christy looked at the bundle and then back at Tucker. "There wasn't any room on our way here. Now what?"

"I can't open the rumble seat and put the gift in there. While that would be the perfect place on a nice day in the summer, the snow and wind would ruin it today." Tucker looked at the bundle and then at his two friends. "Well, Christy, you're the shortest of us." Sizing up the predicament, he added, "Why don't you just sit on the quilt? That might even make you as tall as Johnny and me. And, it would be a really soft ride."

"Well," she said with a smile, "it could be the most comfortable seat in the car."

Tucker carefully smoothed the quilt package and placed it in the middle of the bench seat. The three got into the old Model-A, and Christy crawled on top of the package. She sat back and smiled.

Tucker started the engine, then pulled away from the curb and turned toward the highway. To Tucker, it felt good to be going home. Home was where everything made sense.

One more right turn and they were back on the highway. The shadows were long across the road. With the sky growing darker all the way home, Tucker turned on the headlights. The lamps weren't as bright as in Uncle David's car, but he was able to see the road a little. He drove most of the way at twenty-five miles an hour, to make sure he would be able to see the road in front of him. Once again, Tucker had taken his spot hugging the window, as Christy balanced herself on top of the quilt. That put Johnny half on and half off the quilt. In that spot, he would bounce toward the door every time they hit a bump. But then, every outing with Tucker was a challenge for all those brave enough to go along.

"I like this spot, on top of the quilt," Christy announced with a tone of royal superiority high above the other two. "I can see where we're going from up here."

Tucker laughed. "Don't get too used to it. But, for now, the thick quilt seems to cushion the bouncing of the car. I was watching you guys. I hope you don't hit your heads on the ceiling if we go over much of a bump."

The A Model had just picked up speed when a sleek red sports car flew past them so close Tucker had to jerk the wheel. They were all thrown toward the side window. Tucker gripped the steering wheel, but Johnny landed on the floor. Christy, high on her perch on the thick cushion, bounced back and forth until she landed, piled on top of Johnny.

"Again? Who was that? Do they all drive like crazy people here near the lake." Christy grumbled as she tried to pull herself off the floorboard.

"I don't know who that was, but I'm going to find out." Tucker pushed harder on the gas pedal until he caught up to the sporty red streak at the next traffic light.

Christy and Johnny scrambled to the seat just as Tucker overtook the car when the light turned green, and passed the little vehicle. Inside, a blond kid not more than sixteen years old, and a young girl with flowing red hair, were laughing, and pushing each other in fun.

"The driver doesn't seem to be a dangerous stalker," Tucker concluded. "I'm guessing he isn't one of Manny's so-called family, but I don't give him much credit for intelligence. You just don't play games while you're behind the steering wheel. He's not der gangster. He's der dummkopf."

Still, Tucker had to admit, the two in the red sports car were just kids, just like he was. Tucker already had a really strange day, running into Lana Bertelli. He thought he would never have to see Mannie Bertelli again. But there he was, waving like an old friend. What else was going to happen? But then, Grandpop always said, "Just because something bad happened, doesn't mean the next happening will be bad too."

CHAPTER TWENTY-ONE
Home Again and All Is Well

It was nearly six pm when Tucker pulled the Tin-Lizzie's little sister into the driveway at home. Darkness had completely overtaken the side yard, casting shadows that were created by what was left of the half-moon. The darkness never bothered him before. And, he wasn't going to let all that had happened bother him now. In his mind, he turned the shadows into a yard full of artfully created lawn sculptures.

Tucker already dropped Christy off at her house in time for her evening meal. Mrs. Tree served supper much later than at Tucker's house. But then, the Moyer home was still on railroad time, even though Grandpop had retired years before. Tucker and Johnny headed up the steps onto the side porch.

"You're home." Gramma threw both hands in the air, like a prisoner freeing herself from worry. "I held dinner for you two as long as I could. Tim has been circling around the eggs for quite a while. We had fried egg sandwiches."

"And, cupcakes," Goldie added. "We made the cake Pastor Daily asked for. Your grandfather took it over to the church in the little wagon he said that you and Betsy used to play with. Your grandmother and I baked the cake here, put the layers together and decorated it there. Rebecca thought that would be easier, and believe me, it was." She smiled proudly. "It is a beautiful cake. I'll hate to see it cut into pieces."

"As long as we were making such a big cake," Gramma sighed as she sank into her rocker, "we whipped up some cupcakes too. We had them for our supper and saved one for each of you. I don't know what I would have done without Goldie's help."

"Now, Rebecca, you stay right there in that chair and rock," Goldie said caringly to Gramma. "You've had a very big day. "I'll fry the eggs for the boys."

"Nix, Goldie. You're tired too." Gramma put her hands on the armrest of the chair and started to lift herself off the rocker.

"Now, I'll not hear another word about it." Goldie headed for the kitchen as she kept talking. "I'll have those eggs fried up in no time, then Johnny and I will get out of your way." Over her shoulder, she added, "You two boys wash up."

"Yes, Ma'am," Tucker agreed and motioned for Johnny to follow. He was amazed. There weren't many people who could stand up to Gramma. But then, few tried.

Johnny looked around the room and whispered, "How are you going to get that Christmas gift in the house without your grandmother seeing it?"

"I'll figure it out." In the little bathroom under the stair landing, Tucker picked up the Lava soap from the soap dish and sudsed up his hands. With a squirt of water and lather, he popped the soapy bar over to Johnny. "I have several ways of getting into the house."

"I don't think I want to hear about them," Johnny mumbled with a bit of a shudder. "Seems to me I remember a few."

"Come and get it," Goldie called from the kitchen.

Tucker was hungry. But then, Tucker was always hungry. Earlier, Gramma had also heated up some homemade noodles and added them to a can of homemade chicken broth. Some added seasoning and vegetables made a delicious soup. The egg on Gramma's homemade bread topped the meal off perfectly. There was nothing better than Gramma's homemade bread.

When the war was over, most people started buying their family's bread from the grocery store. Then there was also the baking industry's offering of home delivery. Many neighborhoods enjoyed the luxury of a weekly visit from the breadman. He would pull his delivery truck into a driveway and fill his basket with yeasty-smelling goodies. A knock on the back door allowed those inside to buy their bread and whatever sweet treats caught their eye. Even Gramma had a regular visit from the breadman.

That day, she was expecting Goldie and her son to stay for a light supper. Homemade bread was like a specialty. A year or two back, baking seven loaves of bread every Saturday was a necessity. But now, for a family as large as theirs, one loaf of bread a day was barely enough. Bread with butter lavishly spread on top was a staple of the meal.

"More milk?" Gramma asked Johnny as she slowly limped back into the dining room.

Goldie patted Gramma's shoulder. "Now, Rebecca, we don't need to use up all of your milk."

"I'm fine." Johnny blotted his mouth on his napkin and reached for his cupcake. It was white cake with piles of white icing, sprinkled generously with red and green sugar crystals.

Rebecca went to the refrigerator and took out a milk bottle. "You can't eat a cupcake without milk." She poured an additional half-glass for each of them.

The boys inhaled their dessert, savoring each bite. Even the crumbs were devoured by thumping the end of their finger on top of the smallest nibble. Tucker started to lick his fingers, then saw Gramma watching him and used his napkin.

"I had a wonderful afternoon, Rebecca," Goldie concluded the visit. "The choir had a great rehearsal. We are more than ready for tomorrow evening's service. And, it was fun helping you make that big cake for everyone to enjoy tomorrow night after the Christmas Eve service." She handed Johnny his coat. "You know, since my husband died in the war, staying busy has been my salvation. I would never have been able to be there for Johnny if I hadn't had friends like you and Joseph."

"Thank you, Goldie," Gramma said with a modest smile. "And, without friends like you, I would never have been able to make that cake. I still don't know whether Pastor Daily asked for that cake or if Tucker wanted a huge dessert for Christmas Eve."

Tucker watched as his little grandmother gave Goldie Washington a hug. Gramma had to reach up on tiptoes to wrap her arms around her friend.

"Ma, you'd better rest." Grandpop cautioned her. "I'll go to bed as usual at eight, maybe you'd better too."

"I'm going to read for a while, Pa, so I'll rest. I'll be off my feet. I might even prop them up like everybody tells me." She picked up the book that waited on the side table. "I don't want to miss the Bob Hope show later at eight, just as you go to bed."

Tucker knew Gramma rarely missed one of her favorite radio shows. So, it would be nine o'clock before she would go up to bed. Unless she fell asleep in front of the large, floor-model Philco radio, she would see him go out to the car and bring in her gift. It was already nearly seven o'clock. Tucker wanted to get the Christmas gift in the house before someone found it. Tim might even ask to use the car.

"Uh, Gramma, is Tim out this evening?" Tucker asked, trying to sound casual.

"Ya, Morey Swihart called." Gramma sat back in the rocker. "Tim went with him to a movie. He left right before you got here."

Tucker had to stall until he could quietly slip out of the house. He sat down on the floor and opened the *South Bend Tribune's* funnies section. First, he zeroed in on Dick Tracy, the famous detective with the square jaw. Then Al Capp's comic strip where Li'l Abner was on his job. Abner's responsibility was to cut the small crescent-shape opening in outhouse doors. Tucker wondered what Abner's pay was for the creative work of cutting moon-shaped holes in privies. It really didn't matter. He had never heard of anyone in Elkhart County who had the artful task of decorating outhouses with fancy slots. Those holes, rather moon-slivers or five-pointed stars, let in the light and vented the space.

He read over the entire sheet of funnies, folded the paper, and laid it on the coffee table. "How's the book going, Gramma?"

"Okay, I guess. But I am getting very sleepy." Gramma closed the book, keeping her thumb in the spot where she left off.

How was he going to get Gramma's quilt in before Tim got home if she kept fighting sleep? Tucker wanted the gift to be a surprise to everyone, not just his grandmother. He didn't want Tim to see it either.

"Tucker, will you please get my sewing basket? I'll darn a few socks while *The Chesterfield Supper Club* is on. I might fall asleep before *The Pepsodent Show* starts if I read. Bob Hope will keep me awake."

"I'll get your sewing, Gramma," Tucker agreed and went to fetch Gramma's sewing from the shelf in the closet. Handing her the same sewing basket she had used for years he saw Grandpop straighten a little and put down the *Farmer's Almanac*. His grandfather and Uncle Jacob were beginning to look over the planting season in preparation for the spring garden.

Grandpop finally said, "I'll listen to the *Supper Club,* then I'll go up to bed. I cleaned a lot of snow off the church parking lot to ready it for Goldie's choir." He pulled the Black Diamond liniment bottle from where he had stored it under his chair.

Tucker's heart fell. "I should have been here to help you, Grandpop."

"You helped me all morning, Tucker." With that, Grandpop had spoken. "You're a big help all the time."

Gramma fussed a little with the basket, opening and closing the lid. "I've been thinking, Tucker. I think I'll have you buy some of that Pepsodent toothpaste over at the store. Bob Hope says it's good. I've seen pictures of him in some of the magazines. He has very white teeth."

"Yes," Tucker repeated, "Pepsodent." He was a bit distracted by the brown paper package that waited in his car. "Very white."

Tucker turned the radio up a little. He pretended the increase in volume was for Gramma's benefit. But it also provided a sound cover for any moving around he would have to do to get the quilt inside.

He looked over at Gramma's feet where the dog usually camped out. If Joe wasn't eating or playing a game of tug-of-war with Tucker, he was following Gramma around the house. "Where's Joe?"

Grandpop looked around the sitting room. "He went outside some time ago." The usual nap spots could be seen without him getting up. There was no tail sticking out from behind the end of the couch, and the drapery hung properly with no unsightly bulge. "In fact," he checked the clock on the wall, "he went out when Sam and Sarah left for the evening. That was … over an hour ago."

Tucker's attention perked. "Those two are spending a lot of time together."

Gramma looked up from her darning. "Well, they are engaged." Finally, she had to admit her eyesight was not as good as it was. "Here, Tucker, please thread this needle." She handed the darning needle to him and the thread. "Either my eyes are getting bad, or the needles are shrinking."

"Sure, Gramma."

His grandmother smiled as her eyes softened. "Sarah has been alone a long time, Sam too. It's nice they have found each other, plus a friend to spend time with."

Tucker took the end of the blunt-tipped needle and thread. In one try, he threaded the darning yarn through the eye of the needle and handed it back to his grandmother. "Why is Joe still outside?"

"You know that dog," Grandpop sighed. "He found something to chase, but he'll be back in a while."

Gramma unfolded the blue-diamond argyle sock she was planning to darn and adjusted her glasses. "He ate a while ago, so he's not hungry yet."

"Think I'll go out and look for him." Tucker put on his jacket and started toward the door.

The air outside was cold but crisp and clear. The stars had finally come out and glistened in the winter sky. The moon was in a waxing phase, between a half-moon and full moon. Tucker was fascinated by astronomy. He often leafed through another of Gramma's reference books, *Jayne's Almanac*. The annual publication had pictures and explanations of the phases of the moon. He paired that with other articles he had read, about future flights to the moon, and smiled. His thoughts flitted from the search for his dog to wondering where the man-in-the-moon went when the moon was only half there. He quickly snapped back to the darkened yard but didn't see Joe.

Tucker had been over the exterior of the house and every inch of the yard so many times, that Grandpop said he had given each blade of grass their own name. He could find his way in the daylight and in pitch-black darkness. The window to Tucker's second-story bedroom was always unlocked. He had planned it that way, so he always had a way of getting back into the house if the doors were locked. Gramma usually left the side door unlocked and waited inside until Tucker was in for the night. But, if he was out past the agreed-upon curfew, it might be locked.

That's it. That's what he'd do. He would climb through his bedroom window and hide the Christmas quilt in his closet. Then, he'd go back out the same way, and walk in the side door with Joe.

The sidewalk from the house out to the road was fairly clear following Grandpop's shoveling. But the side lawn to the gravel-covered driveway was still deep with snow and ice. Since his grandfather had never driven a car, he was always more concerned with the footpath than the parking spaces.

Tucker had checked his lace-up, high-top boots before going out. He would not be on the cleared street or sidewalk. He had left the car beside the walk, but he'd have to move it beyond the grass and into the parking area when he retrieved the quilt. Trudging the few steps off the sidewalk to the Ford, the snowy grass and gravel under his feet snapped and crunched with each step. To Tucker, everything about a snowy evening was magical. Then, he heard Joe talking to him in his special dog language from off somewhere. "What is that scamp doing?" he whispered to himself. With each step, the dog conversation was louder. Then, there he was. Joe was sitting on the passenger side of the car, waiting. "Oh, no, Gramma's Christmas present," Tucker moaned.

Joe pawed at the side window and barked louder as Tucker approached the car. Evidence of serious window licking smeared up the glass. Joe didn't seem to have a single guilty expression on his entire list of acceptable mannerisms.

Tucker closed his eyes as he opened the car door. Would Gramma's quilt be chewed beyond recognition? Would dirty paw prints tattoo every square inch of the beautiful tulip tree blossom? With the door open, Joe jumped out and Tucker jumped in. He quickly turned to his dog as the animal's last paw touched the snow. "Stay." A one-word order was all Joe ever needed.

His willingness to obey those in authority was what made him so successful during his years as a WWII war dog. Following orders is how he earned his war medals. Joe immediately folded his hind legs and sat in place. If Gramma or Grandpop came looking for him, it was better that Joe drew his grandparents' attention to the side yard. Tucker still had important work to do.

With one glance, he found the bundle with the paper wrapping. There, tucked behind the driver's seat was the uninteresting beige paper wrapped in binding twine, surrounding a thing of beauty hidden beneath. The paper didn't have the tiniest rip, tear, or tooth mark on it anywhere. Again, he ordered, "Stay," as he reached for a length of rope stashed under the seat.

Tucker watched as Joe sat by the car in the moonlit yard. Using the rope, Tucker wrapped it around Gramma's gift, then looped the whole thing around his chest, like a book bag. Tucker was ready.

He approached the large maple tree in the backyard with a running hop. Throwing his left leg over the lowest branch, he hung upside down until he quickly hoisted himself up to the crook in the tree. In spite of the ice that covered the trunk and branches, from that curve he could shinny out on a limb where he could drop onto the roof of the summer kitchen. Then climbing up Uncle Jerry's old ham radio tower, he would end up on the second floor of the house, and his own bedroom window. He tugged on the frame ... nothing. His window was locked.

Oh no ... Gramma did it again. It had to be her. He definitely did not remember locking the window himself. It was left unlocked for a reason, and he was facing an example of the need at that moment.

Tucker grinned and reached above his window. Using his windowsill as a step, he grabbed the attic window another story above him. He had entered the house in that unusual manner before. With a snap, he pushed the attic window open. Evidently, Gramma hadn't even thought of the attic as a usual entrance to the house. He pulled himself up and through the third-floor window.

Tucker hurried. He didn't want his grandparents to wonder where he was and come looking for him.

In the dark attic, Tucker was thankful the moonlight created a bright path through the middle of the room. Crashing and banging into things could have brought Gramma seeking the cause of the racket with a cast iron skillet in her hand. She didn't raise their first five children all by herself as a helpless female, while Grandpop was away working on the railroad during the week. She knew how to take care of herself, her family, and their home.

With the gift package carefully stashed in the corner of the attic, Tucker hurriedly dove out the window the same way he came in, shinnied down the antenna pole, flipped across the tree branch, landed on the icy ground, collected Joe, and casually walked in the side door. "I found Joe," he announced as he flopped down on the floor in front of the radio. "He had snuck into my car when I opened the door. Never can tell what that dog will do."

CHAPTER TWENTY-TWO

Christmas Eve in the Morning

The light dusting of snow during the early hours of December 24 didn't require a shovel that Christmas Eve morning. Golden rays from the winter sun burned off the most recent deposit of the white stuff. Previous piles might take weeks to thaw. Tucker knew, if it stayed as cold as it was that morning, it would be one of those winters with weeks of old, dirty black snow piled along the sides of the road.

That morning, with no snow to shovel and the table already stretched out for the family Christmas dinner the next day, Tucker wondered how he would spend the morning.

"Christy called," Gramma announced from the kitchen. She was making homemade noodles for Christmas dinner. "You were out playing fetch with Joe when she first rang you up." The rolling pin moved slower and slower as the noodle dough stretched across the flour-dusted counter.

"Are you all right, Gramma?" It was easy for Tucker to notice when his grandmother was in pain. Her face was drawn and her movements tight.

"Ja, sure. I'm fine. Arthritis just caught up to me this morning. I hope I can play the piano for the choir this evening."

Tucker smiled. "Goldie's choir will be here. If you can't play, I might have a substitute for you." He said no more. He knew Johnny was not assertive about anything

... conversation, or piano playing. He watched as his grandmother rolled out the last bits of dough and cut it into long noodle strips. "Can I get your liniment for you?" Tucker was nearly always aware of his grandmother's needs. He worried about her.

"Ja, ist gut. As soon as I finish with these noodles, I'll rub some in my hands. I have to play the piano at the Christmas Eve service this evening. The liniment is on the table beside my bed, Tucker, thanks."

Tucker darted back upstairs and into his grandparents' bedroom. The bottle was right where Gramma said it was: Whitmer's Black Diamond Liniment ... For Man ... For Beast. Manufactured by the H. C. Whitmer Co., Columbus, Indiana. Tucker wondered what beasts the label included.

He laughed to himself. *For man or beast, that covers Gramma and Joe.* He wondered if one of the chickens began to limp if Black Diamond would be the cure for it too. Then he saw a bony chicken foot in his mind and thought maybe there wouldn't be enough skin to cover it with liniment.

The decision of how to dash down the steps was always a challenge. Would he fly like an antelope down the mountainside, or slide down the banister like a ski champion? He would try to be as quiet as possible for Gramma's sake. But he was on a medical mission of health and wellness just for her. He chose to be a distance runner, jumping the hurdles, as he leaped down three steps at a time.

Usually, Gramma and Grandpop didn't say a word about his jumping around the house. If correction was necessary, it often came from Tim or Carolyn. After rearing three boys and two girls in their first family, his grandparents were used to active boys being in the house. When Tucker was dashing through the house or leaping down the steps, Gramma would sometimes grab her head and close her eyes, then continue with her activity.

As Tucker handed her the liniment, she added, "Christy said she was going down to the creek to ice skate about 10."

"Thanks, Gramma. I'll call Freddie." He thought about skating in the frigid air and got excited about the challenge. "I'll see if he wants to walk down there with me."

"You don't have any skates," Betsy reminded him, hearing the conversation as she came into the kitchen. She pulled a cereal box from the kitchen cabinet. "But I do. I might come along. It sounds like fun."

Tim got up from the couch. "Where are you going?"

"Ice skating on the creek," Betsy said as she winked at Tucker. "You comin' too?"

"Ice skating?" Tim shuddered. "I don't think so. But, you two be careful. The ice should be thick, but you never know."

"Will do," Tucker agreed. He watched Tim as his brother stretched and rotated his shoulders. Uncle David told him that Tim had been in a military hospital for a few days when he and his team had an accident with a tank. Tim had pulled them all out of the crash, but it looked like he was still in pain. The VA physicians in South Bend should be able to help him when Tim goes for his appointment after Christmas.

"I have an idea about the skates." Tucker reached for the telephone receiver on the wall-mounted crank phone. "Hi, Carolyn, dial Christy for me, two longs, two shorts, and a long."

Tucker knew his sister, Carolyn, would try to get in as many hours at the telephone office as possible during the Christmas holidays. She was saving for her wedding after high school graduation. It was rumored that the daughter of Dalia, the operator, was sick and would have to go to the doctor before they closed early for the holiday. Dalia was very happy that Carolyn was willing to work as many hours as she could.

"Morning, Tucker," Carolyn greeted as the stand-in telephone operator. "Dialing."

"Hi, Christy," Tucker greeted when Christy picked up the receiver. "Gramma said you called. Betsy and I will meet you at the creek. I'll call Freddie."

"He walked by our house a little while ago," Christy's voice was energized. "He said his mom was sending him to the store for a quart of milk. I'll grab him when he comes back. Freddie can walk down to the creek with me, and we'll see you there."

Tucker finished his call. Then standing in front of the window at the kitchen sink, he washed and dried the bowl he had used for his breakfast. It looked glorious outside. The morning was going to be beautiful.

"Rebecca," Sarah began rather slowly as she slipped quietly into the kitchen, "would you do my hair before the candlelight service tonight? I have that solo and want to look good."

Gramma studied Sarah's long braid. "My hands aren't working very good today. Carolyn will be home around lunchtime. She's really good with hair. She could give you a much younger-looking hairdo than I could."

"That's a good idea," Sam added. "I think you'd like Carolyn's style, Sarah. She reads about all those movie stars in the styling magazines every month. She'll do a nice job."

Tucker's smile broadened and couldn't resist a little tease. "Hairstyles are now your interest, Sam?"

Sam started to open his mouth to answer, then stopped. When Sarah looked at him and returned his smile, Sam went on, "Only Sarah's."

Tucker almost choked on the big bite of Christmas cookie he shoved in his mouth. He wondered why Sarah's hair was so important to the rugged mountain man, but thought he'd mind his own business.

Rattly noises came from the entry hall. What was going on?

When Tucker got there, Grandpop had moved a step stool into the hall closet. He had his foot on the bottom step when Tucker stopped him. Grandpop never thought twice about doing the things he had always done. He even walked around on the roof of the church. But if Tucker was home from school, he tried to scramble to the shingles before his grandfather started up the ladder. Quickly, Tucker asked, "What do you need, Grandpop? I'm right here. I can get it for you."

"Ma said we put the frame for the holly wreath on the shelf in the back of the closet last Christmas. Sarah wants to use it. She's going to weave some white poinsettias blossoms through it. She wants to work on it today." Grandpop stood back and let Tucker do the climbing and searching.

"Did she say why she wanted the flower-covered wreath?" Tucker had already helped put up the Christmas tree and all the holiday nick-nacks that were gathered over years of his grandparents keeping house.

"Didn't ask, but she said she wanted to add it to the sanctuary at the church for this evening's service." Grandpop reached for the wreath frame as Tucker handed it to him. "I've learned to wait and see all the pretty things these women make," he added with a little grin.

"It's a little bent, but I can fix it." Joseph made the frame for Rebecca out of hangers and bailing wire he had gotten from a farmer, so he was the one who could straighten it. He sat down in his Morris chair and began pulling the wires into position with some pliers from the side table.

Grandpop always had pliers or some other small tool nearby. He rode the bus into town one day every week to take care of business. While he was there, he'd wander around the hardware store, enjoying all the "boy's-toys" the store offered. When he got home, he kept the tool near his chair where he could frequently take it out and admire it.

"Okay, Joe." Tucker looked at the dog. "It's time to go skating. Let's go find where you hid them."

"Hid what?" Betsy asked. "Joe buried some skates in the yard? That would be a pretty big hole. I haven't seen anything like that."

Tucker didn't answer the "what," but put on his jacket and started outside. "I'll find them. Betsy, let's go."

• • •

At the creek, Christy was still sitting on a tree stump tying her last skate. "Crackers, Tucker, I wondered when you would get here."

"I was looking for something," Tucker said with a crooked grin. "Joe knew where they were since he had buried them."

Freddie looked down at his own skates and slid them back and forth, testing their smoothness. "Looking for what?"

Betsy rolled her eyes. "Tucker has only said, 'I'm looking for something.'" She found another tree stump where Uncle Jacob had trimmed back trees that were hanging over the creek and threatening to fall in, blocking the flow. Moyers owned the land around the creek. It was part of their original farm.

Tucker reached inside his jacket and pulled out two long bones Joe had gnawed on, and some rope from his pocket. "Joe had buried some beef rib bones we gave him. I guess he planned to dig them up again. They weren't buried very deep. The end of one of the bones stuck out of the ground."

The bones were about twelve inches long, straight in the middle, and curved up a little at each end. Tucker sat down and tied one of the short lengths of rope around each bone at the end and strapped them around his ankle. "Uncle Jacob said these were the first ice skates they used hundreds of years ago."

"He would know," Betsy agreed. "Uncle Jacob reads all the time, everything he can find, and remembers it all." Betsy skated out onto the frozen creek and did a little Bunny Hop step across the ice.

"Wait a minute, Christy," Tucker whispered as he watched Freddie skate out across the icy pond. "Johnny stayed at our house for a sandwich when we got home yesterday. I heard him tell his mom that he had shoveled snow in front of his aunt's store and helped get a lady out of the ditch. His mom said she was glad he was able to help. He didn't call the lady by name. I like his explanation. I don't think Gramma and Grandpop would understand how we got to know a big-time gangster. And, I sure don't want them to stew about it."

Christy checked on Betsy and Freddie's locations. "Tucker, Johnny doesn't really know Lana ... or her husband. None of us do. He probably wouldn't use her name."

Tucker shrugged. "Well, I don't know them either. Bertelli just came in as a customer at the filling station. Then we accidentally stumbled over him at the lake like an old pair of worn-out shoes."

Christy put her hand to her mouth and whispered, "I don't think he would have even touched an old pair of shoes, much less put them on. I told Mom that you bought a Christmas gift for your grandmother at the lake, and we helped a lady dig her car out of the snow."

"That sounds good. It's the truth," Tucker decided. "I won't lie to Gramma and Grandpop. But I don't want to worry them either. We can't help that we found a real-life gangster."

Christy eyed Tucker beneath hooded eyes. "It feels more like, he found us."

Freddie skated slowly past. "Are you ready for the Skating Nationals in those things, Tucker?"

Tucker laughed. "Almost."

Betsy skated up to the edge of the creek as ice chips flew in every direction. "Are you two going to talk or skate?"

"Skate," Tucker announced as he stood up. "Now, let's see if these things work." Tucker put his hand on Christy's shoulder and eased himself across the snow at the edge of the ice.

Christy looked at Tucker's hand on her shoulder. "I'm glad to help, but this may turn out to be a problem. If you go down, Buster, I do too."

"You stay on that side, and I'll take this one," Betsy wrapped a sisterly arm around Tucker's waist. "Okay, Hans Christian Andersen, let's go."

Inching out onto the ice, the rib bones felt strange to Tucker. Once last winter, he had borrowed a friend's pair of fancy lace-up ice skates. His beef bones just didn't feel the same.

At first, the bony skates seemed to have a mind of their own. Then, as Tucker glided past the girls and their comforting shoulders, he cheered for his own accomplishment. "Hey, I'm getting a hang of this."

Betsy circled around and watched Tucker glide across the surface of the ice. "You're looking good, Brother. Strange, but good."

Christy laughed as she kept her eyes on his bony excuse for skates. "Are you ready? I'll race you to the other side."

The two placed their toes on an imaginary start line. Christy couldn't stop laughing at the bones sticking out from the end of Tucker's shoes. Tucker tried not to look at his feet. Bones for ice skates seemed impossible even though he had them on.

Freddie laughed. "Okay, you two. On your mark, get set ... go."

CHAPTER TWENTY-THREE
A Christmas Eve Surprise

When Tucker and Betsy got back from the creek, Tucker was surprised to see Sam's Native American Chief's blanket lying across the back of a dining room chair. Maria Garcia loved that blanket. It would have been her son, Dakotah's, chief's blanket if he had come home from the war. But he hadn't. The tribe had lost a real leader. Why was something so loved and so valuable just lying around?

Or, was Sam leaving to go back out West? He had already stayed longer than the few days he usually stayed under the tree in the backyard, or in the summer house on wintery days. Tucker had heard no talk around the table of Sam going back to the mountains. A few months ago, he had even become involved with the harvest on the farm he still owned a few miles outside of Dunlap. And then there was that shock around the dinner table. He had asked Sarah to marry him. Was she going to move out west and live in a mountain cabin too? Tucker wondered about many things.

Right then, however, everyone in the house was getting ready for the Christmas Eve program. Tucker was certainly not ready, so he'd have to put thoughts of the Chief's blanket in the back corner of his mind. Not that he expected any thought of his to stay buried there. That corner had no lock or any other way to keep ideas from bouncing around like Mexican jumping beans[4]. But he'd deal with that latter. For now, he would forget Dakotah's chief's blanket. It was just part of the memory of Sam Treadway's exciting experiences. He decided, it only lay on the back of a dining room chair by happenstance.

• • •

As the evening began to take over the day, headlights started flooding the church's parking lot when Tucker came back downstairs. He had changed into Christmas Eve clothes, not school clothes, or a Sunday morning suit, but in-between duds.

Grandpop straightened his tie in the hall mirror. If it was a church service, whether Sunday morning or Christmas Eve, for Joseph Moyer, the proper attire for him was his suit and tie.

"Oh ja, Sarah," Gramma sighed aloud and gently touched her new hairdo. "Das ist gut. Real gut."

"Thank you, dear Rebecca." Sarah's hair was ear-length and curled around her face. The dress she had on had to be the one Sam mentioned the other day. Even Tucker thought it was very special, far from in-between duds.

Sam came up behind Sarah, his eyes were warmer than Tucker had seen. "Your solo will be as beautiful as you are."

"Thank you, kind sir." Sarah's face warmed, too, to the point Tucker saw her blush.

Fireworks seemed to be bursting all around, but Tucker didn't know why. Bursts of light rarely happened in their house. Tucker had really only seen them in the movies. Maybe everyone was as excited as he that Christmas was the next day.

"Carolyn," Sarah stopped her as she put on her coat. "Please, don't forget to get a good picture of me during my solo."

"I have my camera," Carolyn reassured her. "I'll take it at the beginning of your song and at the end, so there is little to no movement."

Sarah touched Carolyn's cheek. "And thanks for your amazing talent with hair."

"Everybody, let's go," Betsy announced like the drum majorette in the band. "Coats and gloves on ... hats in place."

They walked across Moyer Avenue together, a family going to church. Snowflakes melted on Tucker's nose and quickly dissolved on his extended tongue.

"Hi, Tucker," Freddie said as he waited inside the door. "Some of the kids are already here. We're all sitting at the back of the sanctuary on the left. Anna is saving me a seat."

"Got it," Tucker answered but kept his eye on a big car that pulled up in front of the corner lot where the new parsonage was being built. Clouds had moved in front of the moon, so it was darker than usual. Still, Tucker could make out an outline and determined that it was larger than most cars in the Dunlap area.

Christy popped into her seat before the entire Junior High Sunday school class had gathered in the sanctuary. The last person to slide into the pew was Johnny Washington. Family, cousins, and friends had gathered for a Christmas Eve candlelight service. Tucker's world was complete.

In the chancel, Tucker noticed Sarah's huge white Poinsettia wreath leaning against the altar. It provided a beautiful centerpiece for whatever was center stage that evening. When the music started, everyone stood, and the combined choirs began their processional to the Christmas carol, "It Came Upon a Midnight Clear." A few worshipers continued to find seats as the choir walked up the center aisle. With the Dunlap congregation and those of the African Methodist church, the room was bulging. Ushers quickly set up additional folding chairs in the space at the back of the sanctuary, behind the pews.

After the evening prayer, the combined choirs got up to sing. Tucker could see Gramma rubbing her hands together. "I'm sorry," Gramma said causally as she stood up and directed her words to the back pews. "Tucker, you said you have a substitute for me?"

"I do," Tucker called from the back of the sanctuary. "Johnny Washington heard all the practices. He could play the piano for you."

Johnny's mouth gapped open as he looked sheepishly around. Then he caught his mother's eyes. She was beaming at her only son. At first, he was hesitant. Then, he hurried forward and slid across the piano seat. Watching as his mother conducted the music, he began.

To Tucker's ear, it didn't sound like the same song they had practiced in the Moyer's living room. There were runs and trills not in the original arrangement. But the words were the same. Goldie and Johnny had composed the lyrics themselves, to the tune of "Away in a Manger."

There's presents and trees and candles galore
Christmas is not about things from the store.

Christ's Day is the birthday of Jesus the Lord,
Bringing love to earth so that we are restored.

When the song concluded and Johnny played the last chords, those in the congregation sang out, "Yes," and "Amen."

Pastor Daily walked to the pulpit. "Thank you, choir. And, especially, thank you Mr. Piano-man, Johnny Washington. You helped to bring the message, which seems to be all that we need." Everyone smiled and nodded. "But, being a minister, I want to add a little more about hope and praise." The pastor continued with a short Christmas Eve message before the elementary-age children came into the sanctuary, dressed in costumes depicting the first Christmas. There were "Oohs" and "Aahs," and a few giggles, as parents and grandparents watched their children with love. Once the children were all in place, the choir rose again to sing, "O Little Town of Bethlehem." Sarah took her place beside the organ for her solo.

It was beautiful. Tucker didn't remember hearing Sarah ever sing a solo before. It filled out the service perfectly.

"Amen," Pastor Daily concluded at the end of the service.

"Wait," a man in the far back called out. "I'm sorry to interrupt such a blessed evening."

Tucker looked back and gasped. Standing in the back was Manny Bertelli. Tucker leaned toward Christy and whispered in a husky voice, "He found us again." Lana sat beside him, all gussied up in frills and diamonds, smiling and waving at Tucker. Two worshipers who were not smiling were Gus and Morty, sitting on the other side of Manny. In fact, they looked like captured prisoners waiting for their turn in front of the judge.

"Your fine young man, Tucker McBride," Manny began again as Tucker thought of hiding under the pew, "helped my wife when she was forced off the road and got stuck in the snow yesterday. We stopped in to thank him and to share the Christmas Eve service with all of you."

The room was quiet. All eyes turned from Manny to Tucker. Bertelli added, "Lana told me that Tucker's helpers are here too, Christy and Johnny." Then he turned toward Morty and Gus. "When I pulled up in front of the house being built next door, which looked to me like a new parsonage, I saw a light in the basement and did a little investigating." He turned to the terrible-two and pointed with a sweeping hand. "I found these two down there where they had hidden a billfold. And, can you believe it, the identification inside, says, Tucker McBride."

Church friends gasped and chattered among themselves. Manny held up his hands to silence the congregation. "Tucker," he said as he walked over to him, "here is your missing billfold. And, for helping my Lana, I stuck a hundred-dollar bill in it for you."

"You didn't have to do that," Tucker drew back. He knew more about who he was talking to than the others did. Being obligated to a man like Manny Bertelli was not a position in which he wanted to be.

"I know I didn't have to," Manny said with a laugh. "I wanted to." Bertelli's opened his palm in Tucker's direction.

Tucker stop protesting. "Thank you, Mr. Bertelli."

"And for your lovely church, I have brought a cash donation. Use it for your parsonage, or any way you think best."

Again, the friends and family together chattered and clapped.

"As for these two," Manny waved a dismissive hand in Gus and Morty's direction. "Do with them whatever you will. I prefer not to stick around until the police come. Lana and I have to leave. We celebrated Christmas Eve with you. We'll be with our family for Christmas day." Manny said no more. He took Lana by the hand, and they left.

Tucker smiled and whispered, "I bet Vinny will be glad he wasn't down in that basement. Maybe he is changing."

Pastor Daily called after Bertelli. "Thank you, Sir."

Sir? Tucker thought. Sir implies knighthood. He's no knight. Manny Bertelli is much more like a nightmare.

CHAPTER TWENTY-FOUR
Let's Celebrate

A hushed wave of mumbling opinions fell over the congregation. Pastor Daily still didn't move from his spot in front of the Poinsettia wreath. His smile seemed to say there was more. "Please, everyone, stay right where you are. I know we have had an unusual service, but we have another event."

Surprisingly, Sarah had removed her choir robe, revealing the special dress she wore. She said it was like a party dress and Tucker agreed. Then, she left the choir loft and took a few steps to the center front of the church. Sam Treadway had quietly moved to the chancel area as well while everyone else was watching the little *Bertelli and Scoundrels Who-Done-it* at the back of the room. Sam had even spread Dakotah's chief's blanket on the floor at the front of the chancel. When did Sam do that? Tucker was baffled. He guessed it was when Manny Bertelli was the center of attention. What was going on?

Pastor Daily nodded at Johnny and whispered something that Tucker couldn't hear. Johnny nodded. Everyone turned their attention to the front as Johnny put his hands on the piano keys. With a burst of the introductory bars to "The Entertainer,"[9] Scott Joplin's wonderful music, Johnny played a little. Then he bounced from ragtime into Felix Mendelssohn, "Wedding March," with a Joplin beat. Tucker recognized both songs, Ragtime, and especially the Wedding March. Gramma had played for every service and most weddings at the church since he was born, and before that so everyone told him. She often taught Tucker little tidbits of musical information from time to time.

Pastor Daily took a small black book from his jacket pocket, and smiled. "Sam and Sarah have come before all of us to be married this evening. With all the wonderful Christmas decorations, the Poinsettias, wreaths, a huge Christmas tree, and the presence of all their family and friends, we invite you to join them in this blessed event. What a beautiful time to celebrate a new beginning for them." He paused and smiled, then opened the book, and read, "Dearly beloved…"

Everyone gasped. Tucker's gulp was far more severe. It sounded more like he choked as he became aware of the independent mountain man's total change in lifestyle. Some of the people even cheered, especially those who knew them well and all they had been through. Gramma clapped her hands, then folded them together in reverence.

When the buzzing stopped, Pastor Daily added, "We have gathered here this evening for several reasons, to praise and celebrate the birth of Jesus and, unknown to you ahead of time, to join Sam Treadway and Sarah Harter in holy matrimony." Pastor Daily continued with the service.

Christy whispered, "Just look around. Their wedding is decorated in Christmas reds and green. It is all so beautiful. Carolyn even brought her camera. How did she know? She's taking pictures of it all, and the wedding couple is right there in the middle of that beautiful wreath."

"Sarah made the Poinsettia wreath." Tucker watched with a wry grin. "Carolyn must have known about the wedding," he whispered. "I bet Sarah told her when Carolyn did her hair this afternoon. Carolyn loves secrets and surprises about beautiful things."

During the wedding prayer, Sam and Sarah knelt on the folded and padded chief's blanket Sam had put in place. All the questions Tucker had, were beginning to be answered. He was moved by the symbolism of blending Sam's old life with the new one he was starting with Sarah. Then his mind wandered off to his parents' wedding. He wondered what that was like. There would have been no chief's blanket, but Tucker liked to think there was something just as special. From what he had been told about his mother, she, too. liked beautiful things and ceremonies. She even grew the grapes, canned the juice, and donated it to the church for use when they had communion.

"And now," the pastor concluded with the grand announcement, "I'd like to present, Mr. and Mrs. Sam Treadway. You may kiss your bride."

"Sam ... kissing in public?" Tucker whispered as he doubtfully shook his head. To his shock, Sam not only kissed his wife in public, he dipped her backward, just like in the movies. Tucker closed his eyes in shock. "I would never have believed it if I hadn't seen it."

"Crackers," Christy sighed with a swoon.

Pastor Daily added with his hand up in a blessing and dismissal, "Mr. and Mrs. Treadway would like for all of us to join them in the fellowship hall for wedding cake and punch. Rebecca Moyer and Goldie Washington baked a wonderful cake. And, it's a big one. Please, everyone, stay. You can finish wrapping Christmas presents when you get home."

Tucker continued in amazement. "Everything was planned right down to a perfect picture of the couple in front of the Christmas wreath, yet no one but the bride, groom, and pastor knew there would be a wedding tonight." He shook his head again. "Gramma didn't even know she was making a wedding cake. She thought she was just making a special dessert for the gathering after the service tonight."

"I salute the three who knew," Freddie said as he straightened and put his hand to his brow. "And I'm ready to try out that cake."

The entire congregation was flabbergasted. But that didn't stop them from clapping, wiggling, gawking, and calling out well wishes as Sam and Sarah walked down the center aisle, followed by the choir in their planned recessional.

"A hundred dollars?" Christy giggled, jumping up and down as she held onto Tucker's arm. "That man gave you one hundred dollars."

"He gave it to us. You and Johnny get some of this, Christy," Tucker insisted. "I couldn't drive and push the car out of the snow at the same time. You both earned your share of the reward money or Christmas gift."

"No," Johnny protested. "He gave it to you."

Tucker rolled his eyes. "Johnny, don't refuse the money. I don't want to be the only one with money in my pocket. And, Manny Bertelli's behavior is not one to copy. His generosity is to be questioned."

"Why?" Christy asked. She had been left out of all the details Tucker had already learned.

Tucker looked around to see who might be close enough to hear. "I told you, Christy. Manny Bertelli is a mob boss."

Christy's eyes and mouth popped open at the same time. "A—"

Tucker put his fingers over Christy's lips. "I told you already."

"It felt like a dream," she whispered and checked to see who was behind her. "It didn't seem like it was true. I blocked it out."

"Thank about your fear of being grounded until you're forty-five, or something like that." Tucker lowered his voice to barely a whisper. "Christy, you remember everything that ever happened."

"Wow, I know." She sat back down, crossed her arms, and clung on tight. "But Lana's sweet personality seemed to erase all of that business about being a Chicago gangster."

"Don't tell anyone," Tucker hushed her the minute the words, Chicago gangster, popped out of her mouth. "I don't know how the church people would feel about taking money from a wise guy."

"Why not?" Johnny asked. "Money is money, just paper. The church didn't promise him anything, It's just cash."

Tucker had to agree with that simple logic. "Johnny, you are a smart fellow. I agree. And, right now, I want cake."

• • •

Tucker watched as Freddie took Anna's hand when they entered the fellowship hall. He nudged Christy. "It looks like Freddie and Anna are getting along just fine. I never knew that Freddie would take anybody's hand unless there was food in it."

"It's cute, isn't it?" Christy said with a wistful smile. "Yet, they are as different as onions and blueberry pie." She looked at the cake and then at Tucker. "I'm surprised you haven't grabbed up a piece yet. The cake has been over at your house."

"It was baked at our house," Tucker explained. "But it was iced, and decorated over here. Gramma figured if it was dropped on the way over, she wouldn't have wasted her time icing it first. Besides, Carolyn isn't finished taking their pictures. I can't snatch up a piece yet. It wouldn't be polite to cut off a wedge before the couple even had a chance to see it."

Christy gave a friendly sock to Tucker's arm. "Hey, I remember last year when you managed to take a small piece out of Lunchbox's chocolate birthday cake. His mom brought it to school after lunch recess while the kids were hanging up their coats. You cut out a sliver with your ruler. Then you pushed it back together and spread the icing over the crack, again with your measuring stick."

"You saw me?"

Christy laughed. "Someone has to keep their eye on you, Tucker McBride."

"Tucker," Birdie Kline, the middle school Sunday school teacher, took him excitedly by the arm. "I am proud of you. You helped a total stranger, Mrs. Bertelli. That's just what the Bible teaches."

"She's either a stranger or your new best friend," Yvonne Sherbet wedged in a nasty tease. "Can you imagine, Tucker? Someone like Manny Bertelli is your buddy."

"Now, Yvonne," Birdie interrupted, "perhaps next Sunday, you could tell the class about the last time you helped a stranger on the road." Mrs. Kline smiled sweetly, but her tone was serious. Then, with a dismissive motion, she turned her back on Yvonne and spoke to Tucker. "I have to get home. I just want you to know that Jesus taught us to help the stranded and alone. That doesn't make them our best friend. That made Jesus our best friend."

"Thank you, Mrs. Kline. I didn't plan on making Manny Bertelli a friend of any kind." Tucker smiled but wondered if Mrs. Kline was right.

Christy glared at Yvonne, waved good-bye to Mrs. Kline, then checked out the cake, and smiled. "I'm glad you couldn't get to this cake, McBride." She stopped and checked the cake again. "Sam and Sarah had a beautiful wedding, and they didn't have to pay a lot of money for decorations or wedding cake. It would be sad if a piece were missing before the bride and groom had a chance to cut it."

"Yep, it was a beautiful wedding, and they saved a lot of money." Tucker couldn't believe how fast things were changing. Sam Treadway, an isolated mountain widow, had just gotten married. And, Carolyn would marry soon too. Gramma had made a big, three-layer wedding cake, yet he wondered how many more fancy cakes would come from her oven. How many more pastries would she be able to create? He wondered how many more Christmases she would enjoy. Then he thought about the Christmas gift he bought for her, and smiled.

CHAPTER TWENTY-FIVE
The Christmas Gift

Tucker always woke up early on Christmas Day. Not as early as Grandpop. Four a.m. was not Tucker's time of day or night. He didn't know what part of the twenty-four-hour-cycle claimed the 4 a.m. hour. Seven was early enough. The day before had been busy. In fact, Tucker always found something to do. He was either playing sports, helping his grandparents or just anyone who happened to need help, working for Butch, or any of hundreds of possible activities. He did not just sit around doing nothing. Tucker was never bored.

From Tucker's bedroom window, he could see a light snow falling, mixed with showers, and patches of shallow fog. He knew the fog would burn off as soon as the sun warmed the morning. He sat up and found Joe's nose lying near the foot of the bed. The dog knew better than to jump up on the bed. Gramma didn't permit that. Sheets were only replaced when absolutely necessary. And, a dog didn't need to increase the necessity. But no one had said, "Down boy" when he laid only his head on the blanket.

"Well, good morning, Joe." With his hands on both sides of the dog's head, Tucker scratched Joe's ears and rubbed his nose down across the dog's muzzle. "A very Merry Christmas to you."

A blue plaid long-sleeve shirt draped over the back of the chair waited in the corner, along with his best blue jeans, and a clean undershirt. He chose his wool socks and clodhoppers for the morning. If the snow began to fall heavy again, he might have to help shovel the walk. Also, with company coming, the parking area needed to be cleaned. Although, with the church's parking lot just across the street, there were plenty of parking spaces.

He thought he might fly down the stairs, three steps at a time, like usual, but thought of Gramma. With all the family coming for dinner and gift-giving, the day would be a joy, but also stressful for her. She'd be on her feet all day. Tucker already knew that her hands were aching and swollen. She'd be exhausted before the Christmas party was over and all the family would leave.

Downstairs, in the kitchen, Gramma had just poured a cup of coffee. "I was shocked," she whispered to Grandpop. "Shocked and thrilled at the same time. My head felt wobbly."

Grandpop sipped from his cup as he looked out the window. "Sam told me the other day, the people who rented his farmhouse had moved out. I thought they had just found another place to live. I had no idea that Sam was getting married and would move into the house with his wife. I had even less notion that he was getting close to Sarah before the big announcement." He shook his head and gave Gramma a little hug around her waist. "The snow keeps falling."

"No one told me anything about a wedding." Gramma wiped the counter off with a red and white dishcloth she had knitted years before. "And I never guessed that the fellowship dessert was a wedding cake."

Grandpop shrugged. "Last week, I asked Sam why his tenants moved out so fast. Sam said it wasn't that the

Martin family had other plans. Sam simply had another use for the house. He didn't say more, so I didn't ask."

Gramma covered her mouth and chuckled mischievously. "I know his plans now … he did have another use for the house. At the reception, Sarah said they had been cleaning and painting Sam's farmhouse all week. She told me that she and Sam have plans to move their stuff out of here into the house after the Christmas dinner today, or sometime tomorrow." She paused a moment. "You know, with everybody that will be here today, they could all load up a few things in each car and drop them off at Sam's on their way home."

Grandpop drank the last swallow from his coffee cup and put the mug in the sink. "Ma, you go in and sit down and rest. I'll go over and bring back some of the folding chairs from the church."

"I'll help you, Grandpop," Tucker spoke up. He'd eat his breakfast cereal later. Besides, there were plenty of Christmas cookies in Gramma's crock. And, there was always plenty to eat at family holiday meals. All the aunts brought their favorite main dishes, side dishes of corn pudding, green beans, and as many desserts as there were hands to bring them in. Gramma often bought a ham from Maynerd's Meat Market in Goshen. In recent years, the family had gotten so big, the ham had to grow too. Besides the store-bought ham, the company where Uncle Jacob worked gave each employee a gift of a Christmas ham. Grandpop carried Jacob's ham down into the summer kitchen, so Gramma could cook it in the large, old, wood-burning, cookstove[5]. The other ham fit nicely in the kitchen stove.

"Joseph, don't be silly," Gramma protested. "I don't need to rest yet. I just got up a few hours ago."

Grandpop waved her off. "Go … sit … listen to Christmas music; read your Bible; close your eyes. We'll be back soon. I know you aren't exhausted yet. The rest is to build you up before you get worn down."

Once they put on their coats, hats, and gloves, Tucker and his grandfather trudged across the street to the church. The door would be locked since there were no services on Christmas day. Christmas was the day for families, just like that first family in Bethlehem. Grandpop pulled the key from his pocket, turned it in the lock, and stopped as soon as they were inside.

"Tucker, wait. Let's talk. Milo Boxman stopped me last evening after the service. He told me what happened the other day. He said you met Manny Bertelli at Butch's filling station before you ever found his wife by the side of the road, and helped her out of the ditch. Manny Bertelli was right here in Dunlap, across the street from our house. Boxman said Bertelli is a mob boss."

"Yep, so it seems." Tucker headed toward the nearest classroom for chairs.

"I'm proud of you, Tucker," Grandpop assured him as he followed. "It sounds to me like you handled everything as best you could." Grandpop folded a few more chairs and toted them into the hallway.

Tucker hefted four chairs under each arm. "Bertelli already knew I live in Dunlap, because, like you said, he stopped first at Butch's station. Other than that, I didn't give him any other details. He doesn't know I live just across the street."

Grandpa sighed in relief. "Ja, Tucker, you finished that guy for sure. Das ist gut."

• • •

Christmas dinner was everything Tucker had waited all morning for it to be. Each aunt brought whatever they enjoyed to take home as leftovers. Tucker was glad Aunt Karen brought the same cranberry salad she made for their Thanksgiving dinner. It was always a big hit. But that wasn't all she brought. The cherry on top was an appropriate cake she called Carnival Dessert. It was red for Christmas, with bright red cherries in it, and a warm cherry sauce on the top.

Aunt Franny was always very practical. She knew Gramma baked a ham, but she added to the variety of food by bringing a hamburger chopped suey dish. She knew her five children and assorted grandchildren liked it. And warmed up later it made the perfect snack for Uncle James.

Gramma's special-made noodles, cooked with her own beef broth, filled a bowl. Scattered around among the tasty long, flat pasta were bits of beef for added flavor. She had saved the beef pieces from the roast she had fixed a few days before. The back corner of the refrigerator, behind a large jar of dill pickles, was usually the safest place to stash the food she was saving.

Aunt Cora also brought two dishes: two loaves of homemade whole wheat bread were the first treat. All the Moyer children and grandchildren liked bread. They all learned to make bread when they were still quite young. Since Uncle Jerry was reared Amish, Aunt Cora had some great recipes, and Amish Custard was the treat she brought that Christmas day.

Christmas sugar cookies were baked and iced by several of the families. Each baker had their own turn on a special holiday cookie. In Tucker's estimation, no dinner could have too many Christmas cookies cut in the shape of trees and Santas.

Dishes of scalloped potatoes, garden-grown and freshly canned butter beans, and homemade strawberry preserves and grape jelly from the vines in the side yard, filled out the loaded table with food.

As with every meal in the Moyer home, eating didn't commence until the Lord had been thanked for all the blessings He showered upon them. Blessings of wealth? No. Gold in the Moyer family was weighed in hearts full of love, not in rocks from the ground. Even though David was a pastor, it was Grandpop who offered the prayer of grace.

Tucker knew the words would be the same. They always were. But then, so was Grandpop, the same, dependable man of God. The repetitiveness didn't make the words boring. It made the words in the prayer easier for Tucker to remember and bury in his heart.

Everyone became silent as they bowed their heads and waited for Grandpop. "Our kind heavenly Father, again we return thanks to thee for the privilege of being permitted to surround this table blessed by thy bountiful hands. Bless this food to its intended use. Fit and qualify our hearts to thy service. In Christ the Redeemer's name. Amen."

"Now, everyone," Uncle David announced, "find a spot to sit. All the children can sit on the floor, under the table, or in the closet if that's where you will be comfortable."

Tim held up a finger for permission to speak. "Am I still a child, or do I actually get to sit in a chair?"

David laughed and said, "You have earned your spot as an adult, Tim. If there aren't enough chairs, I'll sit on the floor, and you can have my seat."

Tucker smiled as he saw his brother with different eyes. He was a military man, not a tease. "If there isn't a chair for you, Tim, I'll go back over to the church and bring over a few more."

"Thanks, Tucker," Tim softened. "And if we need more, I'll help you get them."

There wasn't a formal setting at the table. The dining room table was loaded with food. Some of the youngest cousins sat cross-legged under the table. This year, Tucker felt more mature. He had actually met the godfather of the Chicago mob and had handled himself well. So, he and Luke took their plates to the stairsteps, sat on one, and used the step above to rest their plate on. Betsy joined them as they stretched up the stairs. There was more food in one place than Tucker had seen since the Thanksgiving family feast. He went back for seconds and then thirds before deciding he was full.

After everyone had eaten, Uncle David and Uncle Jerry had taken on the role of chief bottle-washers. While each family had brought their own place servings in a picnic basket or brown paper bag, no one wanted to pack up dirty dishes. As soon as one of the family finished eating, the men started gathering up the dishes. They would not leave Gramma with a kitchen full of dirty dishes. Betsy and Carolyn helped by drying the clean plates. They knew which place settings went in what cabinet, and which family would claim their own plates and utensils.

Except for the constant deposit of cookie crumbs, sticky fudge-covered fingerprints, re-filled coffee cups, and punch glasses, the kitchen was clean. Finally, all the family gathered around the large Christmas tree in the living room. Younger cousins wiggled, giggled, and waited anxiously. Tucker had grown past that. But he wasn't past a third helping of Aunt Karen's cranberry salad. There in the living room, he left the chairs for grown-ups and found a spot on the floor in front of the radio. With a fork in one hand and a small fruit bowl in the other, he finished off the last bite of apples and oranges in the cranberry salad. Suddenly, he stopped and nearly choked. He left Gramma's Christmas present in the attic.

As fast as he could go, he darted into the kitchen, deposited his cranberry dish in the sink, then flew up the steps, three at a time, dodging a full array of cousins still finishing their dessert on the steps. Down the hall and in through his closet door, he pulled back the clothes that hung at the far end and climbed the few steps to the attic. There it was. The package, wrapped in drab light brown paper and tied with string, was exactly where he left it.

He dashed to the corner where Gramma's collection of used ribbons, cards, and paper were stored and pulled out the bag. Rummaging through to the bottom of the bunch, he grabbed a large gold ribbon. Using a small piece of string he found in the sack of wrappings, he tied the colorful bow to the top.

Tucker didn't feel his feet touch any of the steps all the way back down from the attic. Once he was in the upstairs hall, he could hear Uncle Jacob playing his violin in preparation for gift-giving.

"Carolyn, why don't you accompany Jacob on the piano," Gramma suggested. "That would be a real treat."

With a roll of the backs of her fingers on the keyboard, Carolyn began "Here Comes Santa Clause" with Uncle Jacob fingering trills beside her. "Right down Santa Clause Lane," Tucker joined in as everyone sang along.

In 1947, there weren't expensive presents in the stacks of colorful packages under the tree. And certainly not with Grandpop's eighty dollars a month pension[5]. Gramma had crocheted a monogram in the corner of a white handkerchief for each of the men, and a fancy border on a hankie for each of the women. Gifts back to Gramma and Grandpop were different. The aunts and uncles bought things like a new teapot and a special necktie for their parents.

Tucker hadn't re-wrapped Gramma's gift. It was still in the tan-colored paper but now boasted a colorful top, burying the mailing twine beneath. That was still better than if Tucker had left the package drab and colorless. He checked the wall clock. It was almost three. Good. Christy and Freddie said they were going to stop by. With smaller families, their Christmas dinner and gift exchanges were over, and the discarded wrappings picked up by that time. Tucker's friends wanted to be there when Gramma opened the gift. They felt like they had contributed to the present, too, by just being there when Tucker bought it. Being with Tucker was always a challenge.

Just then, someone tapped on the door. When it opened, Christy walked in. "Hi," she called out. "Merry Christmas."

"Come on in, Christy." Tucker was glad she was there. Well, Freddie too. But Christy and Tucker had been glued together since they were little.

"Mrs. Moyer," Christy handed her a handmade Christmas card. "I made this for you and Mr. Moyer."

"Oh, child, it is lovely." Gramma opened the card decorated with a plump Christmas tree on the front and read the verse Christy had written.

To: Mr. and Mrs. Moyer - 1947

May the sun shine bright upon your face. May angel wings, each tear erase.

From: A Christmas Tree.

"Das ist gut, Christy, Miss Christmas Tree." Grandpop touched the card gently with gnarled and worn fingers. "Ma will put it in her Bible."

Tucker couldn't believe it. Christy had created something very special again. It seemed to him she always knew what to make.

He slipped into the hall and rummaged in the back of the coat closet. Not only was his class project there, it was still tucked under the pile of old jeans and shirts. Tucker had moved it from the attic during the night. He pulled it out and took it into the living room. This year, he had two presents for his grandparents.

"Grandpop. Mr. Justine graded my class project, so he brought it home, and I picked it up at his house. I'd like you to have it for Christmas." He placed the stool on the floor in front of Grandpop's Morris chair. Looking at the chair and stool together, Tucker realized he had succeeded in his design, creating it very much like an Amish Mission stool out of red oak and brown maple. Slats down the sides of the stool supported a dark brown leather cushion on top. "No matter where you sit, you will have a footstool to put your feet on."

"Tucker, this is wonderful." Grandpop ran his fingers over the silken finish of the wooden legs and the tufted leather on the top. "You finished it off beautifully."

Tim had been sitting quietly against the wall. He stood up and looked over the heads of the kids sitting in front of him. "Tucker, you finished your project even before time and did a great job. Good for you."

Everyone smiled and whispered about the workmanship of the footstool. The chatter and praise coming from the family were soothing salve to Tucker's soul. He had completed what he started, two times over.

"Gramma, I got a present for you too." Tucker handed her the large non-descript package with the dull, uninteresting paper and bright gold bow.

Tim was still on his feet in the corner of the room. "Wow, little brother."

Christy knelt on the carpet beside Gramma's chair. Her eyes danced. "Johnny and I were with Tucker when he bought the gift. I can't wait for you to open it."

"I heard it was quite a day," Freddie joined in. When he saw Tucker's slight negative shake of his head, he stopped. A Christmas party was not the time or the place to bring up Manny Bertelli's name.

Gramma held the package on her lap and turned it around, looking for an opening in the wrappings. "I won't tear the paper off. It's too pretty."

Several of the family mouthed the word, but not out loud. "Pretty?"

The binding twine was tied at the top, still forming the backpack that helped Tucker bring the package into the house. Gramma finally found a loose end in the paper and pulled. When the wrapper finally fell away, the beautiful yellow tulip tree blossoms on a field of mint green smiled from the top of the fabric. Leaf-shaped foliage bordered the entire quilt.

"Tucker," Gramma gasped. "Oh, my goodness, Tucker. It is beautiful. I have never seen anything like it. How …?"

His chest puffed out. "Work, Gramma. I bought it at a little store up at the lake. In fact, Johnny Washington's aunt owns the store." Suddenly, he realized that he had actually completed the work he had set out to do. He had completed both the stool and the work at Butch Randolf's Sinclair station. "I earned the money, Gramma."

"That is the best Christmas present you could have given me, Tucker," Gramma said as she reached out and took his hand. "A gift from your heart and your own hard work is always very special."

CHAPTER TWENTY-SIX
A Christmas Gift - New Beginnings

The family Christmas celebration was nearly over. It was late in the afternoon when the board games were picked up and stored until the next time someone pulled them out of the back of the closet. Monopoly and Uncle Wiggily were placed on top of the stack since they were the most popular. Uncle David gathered all the discarded wrappings into one large sack for the burn barrel out beyond the sleeping garden in the backyard. But Gramma liked to save the bows and ribbons to be used another time. As Tucker knew, she had a special bag in the attic for carefully smoothed wrapping paper, bows, and Christmas cards. Tucker had already used a bow from the stash that very day. The third-grade Sunday school class used cut pieces of the old cards and pasted snippets of ribbon to create fresh new cards for parents and grandparents the following year.

Tucker, Uncle Jerry, and Luke were just finishing off Gramma's cherry pie. No one could make a cherry pie like Rebecca Moyer. There was something special about it. Since Tucker didn't bake, he had no idea what it was that made it so good, but he did know how it tasted – fantastic. He scrapped every crust and crumb from his plate with the side of his fork and finally had to admit to himself that the piece of pie was gone. He gathered up the last three pie plates, washed them with Vel Dishwashing soap, rinsed off the soap, and placed them in the dish drying rack.

"Okay, listen up," Uncle David announced. "Sarah stored some furniture pieces in the loft of Dad's workshop. James and Franny, you two go out there and see what you can take out to the farm. I'll get the rest."

Tucker watched as David whispered to Aunt Franny and Uncle James. He wondered why there were so many secrets about things that didn't need to be hushed.

David bent over and whispered to Cora and Jerry. "Sarah said she has some table lamps and floor lights in the basement. I think they will fit in your car. Be really careful. Sarah said one is a Tiffiny lamp. I understand it could be very expensive. I don't think she would want the others to know they had invested in such an extravagance."

Cora leaned in and whispered back, "They didn't buy it, David. Someone from one of their churches gave it to them."

"Oh," David nodded, "that's different."

Tucker had to wonder what was so different about it. An expensive living room lamp was okay if it was given but not purchased? Another question with no answer.

"If we can't get it all in the car on the first trip," Jerry offered, "we'll make a second one. We'll get it there."

"Karen and I will load up Sarah's bedroom suite," David offered. "I was able to borrow a truck from a neighbor. Jacob, if you squeeze Tim, Carolyn, and Betsy in with you, I can also load Sarah's sheets and bedding in the truck. The neighbor, Adele Stuart, said she and her husband would take Mom and Dad. They would love to see Sarah and Sam's house."

Tim straightened his back like a true Marine. "Uncle James, I can help bring some furniture out. And, Uncle David, if any of the pieces need to go into the truck, I can lift them up for you to position inside."

"Thanks, Tim. You have matured, young man." Then David turned to Tucker. "Tucker, you, and your friends can put Sarah's boxes of dishes from the summer house into the rumble seat of the Model A. If Christy and Freddie want to ride out too, they can sit up front with you. I think they might fit."

Tucker and Christy looked at each other and smiled. Christy boasted, "I think we've already proven that we can get three of us on the bench seat."

"If it's okay with your parents," David said to the cousins, "you can ride in the back of the truck on top of the blankets. The truck is covered. I'm not going to drive you around the neighborhood in an open truck bed."

Everyone had their assignment. What might have taken Sarah and Sam hours to pack and load up, the family had it on the way in short order.

• • •

Sam's farm was only three miles out of town, past the bridge over the creek and then off to the left. It sat on forty-four acres with a four-acre stand of woods at the end of the lane. Besides the house, there were several out-buildings. When everyone began turning into the farm's drive, they first saw a large red barn in the center of the yard. Although it stood back from the road, its impressive size dominated the barnyard. An old, unused chicken coop, was up against the fence along the right side of the property. Between the barn and the home, was a fieldstone milkhouse with a green shingle roof.

215

As usual, Tucker was quickly distracted by the little building and wanted to see the inside of the rock structure. "Come on," were the only two words Tucker used. With a small wave of his hand, like he was erasing a to-do list from a classroom blackboard, he made a beeline for the milkhouse. There was no lock on the door, and it opened easily. Along one wall was a built-in deep trough to hold cooling water. Although it was obvious by the invasion of spider webs that the milkhouse hadn't been used in years, a pump was still attached to the side. Tucker imagined that the Moyer pitcher pump would make filling the trough easy. Empty ten-gallon milk cans were in the concrete trough. The milkhouse would have kept the family's milk supply cool for hours. Or the cans would have waited there for the local dairy truck to stop by the farm and pick up the huge, twenty-five-gallon milk drums to process and sell to stores.

"Isn't this amazing?" Tucker asked in awe. "Freddie, you and I would have built a clubhouse out of this little building."

"If you remember, McBride," Christy sassed with her hands on her hips, "I was a card-carrying member of the Dunlapers Club too."

"You sure were," Freddie admitted enthusiastically. Tucker pulled Christy's hat down over her forehead. "Just one of the guys."

Christy yanked off her stocking cap and shoved it into her pocket. "They have the door open now, Tuck. You're wandering from the mission at hand, my friend. Let's get the boxes of dishes out of the back of your car and go in."

"Yes, Ma'am," Tucker snapped to attention and accepted his re-assigned task with a small salute.

As each car parked in the barnyard, they began to unload their cargo. Sam and Sarah brought in the chief's blanket and assorted boxes of things Sarah had gathered since she moved in with Rebecca and Joseph. She had stored each precious keepsake, including her small jewelry box, in low boxes under the bed.

Tucker carried one side of the large box of dishes and Freddie hoisted the other. They were glad the kitchen was ready for them, freshly painted, clean, and ready to fill. He looked around at the small room and smiled. "Sam said he and Sarah had painted the kitchen cabinets inside and out, and the same with the drawers. So, it should be ready for us to put the dishes and silverware away."

The main door along the west side of the building opened into the kitchen. It was easy to see it was the main entrance. The sidewalk led up to the side porch and the kitchen door first, before it wound around to the front of the house.

"Thank you for bringing all of that stuff in," Sarah said as she came through the kitchen. "You three decide where the dishes and silverware should go and put them all away. I have quite a few spices, so shelve them someplace. If I find a better arrangement after we've settled in, I'll change it later. Right now, it would be a real blessing to have it all stashed and all the empty boxes moved out."

"Sure, Sarah," Tucker agreed in amazement. After she went into the living room, Tucker whispered to Christy and Freddie, "Gramma would never have let anyone set up her kitchen for her. She would want it *just so*."

"But, Tucker," Christy reminded him, "Sarah's husband, Steven, was a minister. They moved a lot over the years. She never lived in her own house. They lived in parsonages. I imagine she got so she really didn't care where things were. She would be moving in a few years anyway."

"I didn't think of it that way," Tucker admitted.

They sat the box of dishes on the blue linoleum countertop. Sam had said he bought the piece of linoleum, with a colorful pattern of small ribbon strips, cut, and installed it on the counter himself.

Uncle David and Aunt Karen came in and added a few more cartons containing cast iron skillets, a tea kettle, an electric coffee pot, and other cooking vessels David had hauled in the truck.

"Wow," Christy whistled, "the kitchen is our blank slate. We can put things wherever we want to."

"Then, let's start writing on our slate," Tucker concluded. "Christy, you're the future homemaker here. You have probably worked in the kitchen more than Freddie and I have, helping with meals and baking cookies. What do you think Sarah would want in the upper cabinet beside the sink? We'll start there."

"Water glasses," she concluded decidedly. "I have an idea. Just get a mental picture of your grandmother's cabinets in your mind and recreate the shelves here."

"Good idea. Freddie, you work up here and we'll do the drawers." Tucker opened the top drawer and stepped back. "Well, this is perfect."

"This will be easy," Christy said with a smile. The inside of the drawer was partitioned into separate sections for knives, forks, spoons, and other utensils. Sarah had already lined each section with colorful shelf paper in a yellow rose pattern.

Tucker and Christy filled the compartments with silverware while Freddie began to shelve the dinner plates and coffee mugs in a cabinet above, also lined with the same shelf paper. Pots and pans were placed in lower cabinets, serving dishes in the upper. The many spice boxes were stacked in the upper cabinet beside the stove opposite the dishes.

When the drawers and cabinets were full, Tucker smiled. Not only had he taken on a task, he had helped to complete the job with pride.

"It looks good, McBride." Christy gave Tucker a little sock in the arm. "Now, let's check out the rest of the house."

The lamps that Cora and Jerry brought to the farm sat on the end tables that David and Karen delivered to the living room. The Tiffany lamp, with its stained-glass shade in colors of yellow and green, was on a table in front of the large window. The house was coming together rapidly.

"Mrs. Stuart, Merry Christmas." Tucker greeted his next-door neighbor as she came into the room with Gramma and Grandpop. Adele Stuart and her husband were always nearby and available to help.

"Merry Christmas to you too, Tucker," Adele said with a broad smile as she looked around the room. "Rebecca, this is going to be lovely for Sarah and Sam."

"Ya, lovely," Gramma agreed as she walked through the living room.

Grandpop rubbed Tucker's shoulder. "I know it worried you when a few people teased about Manny Bertelli. Tucker, your boss told you to pump gas for his customers. That doesn't mean you were making best friends. It means a friendly young man was doing his job."

"Look, Pa." Gramma pointed to a blank wall on the south side of the room. "It can hang right there."

"Here, Tucker, you take the hammer." Grandpop handed him a tack hammer he had brought from his workshop at home.

Gramma stopped when Sarah came into the room. "Here's the picture we talked about this morning, Sarah. I thought it would fit nicely here on this wall."

"Rebecca, it will be lovely there." Sarah touched the surface of the oil painting and smiled. "Tucker, I see you have the hammer. Hang the picture at eye level, please. My eye height, not the tallest man in the circus."

"Yes, Ma'am." Tucker tacked the picture hanger to the wall and adjusted the wire on the back of the painting. He hung it exactly where Sarah wanted it.

Surrounded in a wide, red-maple frame was a painting of autumn along the Susquehanna River near Enola, Pennsylvania, in Cumberland County. Sarah couldn't stop taking in the beautiful picture. "The Moyer family farmed in that area of Pennsylvania even before the railroad came in, and before Enola became an official town. But I certainly remember that beautiful river and all the colors in the fall. My parents and I visited Enola when I was in my teens. Our people had lived there for years too."

"The painting is beautiful, Sarah," Christy said as she admired the work.

"Rebecca," Sam began as he joined the family near the painting, "the picture of Sarah and Joseph's original family home-place is amazing. Thank you. It is just the thing to help start a new beginning, knitting our families together."

"That's what Christmas does, Sam." Gramma smiled and turned. "Just like your Christmas present, Tucker. You knew what you wanted to get, and you followed through, pulling the joy of Christmas together for all of us."

It finally occurred to Tucker. At Christmas, we celebrate Jesus's birthday not because of bicycles and new blue jeans. But because of the gifts he brought to us. Tucker realized a special one, the gift of new beginnings.

Addendum

Grandma and Grandpa Kime (Moyer) were very generous with their home. Sarah Harter (Aunt Mary Reigel) did live with the family for a time after her husband died. However, her stay in the house was not at the same time Tucker McBride (Bill Rapp) and his siblings lived there. She shared their hospitality before the children came to live there. Perhaps when their first family was young. My husband (Bill) was not sure of those dates.

Uncle Jacob (Jules Kime) was their bachelor uncle who lived in the house. Jules was their mother's older brother, and since he had a steady job, he was their legal guardian. A quiet man, he was the "parent" who took the children to the doctor and dentist. With their Aunt Ruth and Uncle Dan down the street, Uncle Dwight and Aunt Grace a few doors down another street, and cousins close by, it did take a community to rear Tucker McBride (Bill Rapp).

Tim McBride (John [Jack] Rapp) was in the Marines and worked on and drove tanks. However, he did not go in right after WWII. Jack was in the Korean War. He earned The Purple Heart and another medal.

Sam Treadway (Christian [Chris] Hollinger), another cousin, did come occasionally for a brief visit. Bill found him to be fascinating. However, he and Sarah (Mary) didn't marry, nor were they there at the same time. They are included here as examples of Bill's grandparents' generous nature and willingness to open their home to others in need.

While members of the Chicago mob did come to the lake to get away from "the heat" in the Chicago area, there was no contact with the Moyer family. The area "gossip" placed the gangsters in the lake area much earlier, before World War II, during the prohibition era.

Glossary

[1] "Let it Snow." 1945. Sammy Cahn and Jule Styne. Hollywood, California.

[2] "Toot, Toot, Toosie." 1922. Lyrics by Gus Kahn, Ernie Erdman, and Danny Russo.

[3] Al Capone (Scarface) - was a Chicago gangster who came to the public's attention during Prohibition. He was the co-founder and boss of the Chicago Outfit in the late 1920s.

[4] Mexican Jumping Beans. Seed pods that have the larva of the small "Cydia saltitans" moth. When the larva moves, it makes the bean "jump."

[5] Coal-burning Cookstove

[6] $80. The salary per month in 1947 is equal to $1,104.36 a month in 2024. $1,104.36 per month computes to a 2024 annual salary of $13,252.32 - for Gramma, Grandpop, and the four children. Uncle Jacob often brought in food and paid for items necessary for the children's use at school.

[7] 1893 World's Columbian Exposition in Chicago.

[8] Whirligigs

[9] Joplin, Scott. 1902. "The Entertainer." John Stark & Son of St. Louis, Missouri. (In the 1910s it was sold as piano rolls to be played on a player piano.) Joplin also composed "Maple Leaf Rag."

[10] 1941 Willys Americar 

Recipes

Chop Suey

Preheat oven at 350º

Brown: 1 ½ pounds lean hamburger

One small onion

1 cup celery

In 9x13 x2 inch baking pan, Mix together:

1 cup minute rice

1 can cream of mushroom soup undiluted

1 can cream of chicken soup undiluted

3 ½ cups boiling water

5 tablespoons soy sauce

1 tablespoon brown sugar

Mix in browned hamburger and vegetables.

Bake at 350º for 45 minutes

Last 15 minutes, top with 1 can Fancy Chow Mein Noodles and return to oven.

Whole Wheat Bread

Makes 2 loaves   Preheat oven to 350°

Soften   1 packet active dry yeast in ¼ cup warm water

Combine in a large bowl:

     ½ cup firmly packed brown sugar   1 tablespoon salt

     3 tablespoons shortening   1 cup boiling water

Add: ¾ cup cold water.

     Cool to lukewarm. Stir in the softened yeast

Add gradually:

     4 cups whole wheat flour

     1 ½ to 2 cups All Purpose flour until dough

Knead   on slightly floured surface until dough is
smooth and satiny — about 7–10 minutes.
Place in a greased bowl — cover

Let rise   in warm place (85° to 90°) until light and double in size, about 2 hours

Punch dough down — Let rise 30 minutes

Divide dough in half. Shape into rounded or long loaves and place on greased cookie sheets or in two 9x5x8 inch long pans. Cover

Let rise in warm place until light and double in size — 1 ¼ to 1½ hours

Bake at 350° for 50 to 60 minutes. Remove from pans immediately

Sugar Cookies

(Author's grandmother's [Bertha Naomi Musselman Bryson] 1945 recipe. Grandma Kime also made cut-out Christmas cookies every year.)

Preheat oven to 400°

2 cups shifted flour

1 ¼ teaspoon baking powder

¼ teaspoon salt

⅓ cup corn oil

¾ cup sugar

1 teaspoon vanilla

1 egg plus milk to make ⅓ cup

Sift flour, baking powder, and salt into bowl. Add oil. Blend well with fork or pastry blender. Mixture will appear dry. Beat sugar, vanilla, and egg mixture together until light and fluffy.

Stir into flour mixture. Chill about 1 hour. Roll out on a floured board or cloth. Cut into desired shapes.

Before baking, place nuts on cookies or sprinkle with colored sugar.

Bake in a 400° oven about 9 minutes.

Homemade Noodles

    2 large eggs

    ¾ teaspoon salt

    3 tablespoons milk

    1 ½ - 2 cups All Purpose flour

• Mix eggs, milk, and salt until smooth. Stir in 1 cup flour until smooth. Add the rest of the flour, a spoonful at a time, until dough makes a ball. It will still be slightly sticky.

• Turn dough out onto a floured surface. Flour hands and knead dough until no longer sticky = 3-5 minutes. Cover with clean tea towel. Let dough rest for 10 minutes.

• Roll dough out on a lightly floured counter, parchment paper, or bread board until thin, less than ¼ inch thick or paper thin.

• With sharp knife or pizza cutting wheel, cut noodles into long strips to your desired width: narrow or wide.

• Allow them to dry on a clean tea towel or dry across cooling rack. Air dry for 2 hours.

• You can cook them immediately by adding to a pot of boiling water and cook until tender, about 10-12 minutes. Drain and serve in your favorite recipe. Or, drain and add butter. Sprinkle with parmesan cheese if you like.

• Or seal in an airtight container and keep in refrigerator a few days. Or completely dry and keep in an airtight container for up to a month. The noodles will snap when broken when completely dry.

Carnival Dessert (Cherry Cake)

½ cup shortening

1½ cup sugar

2 eggs

2¼ cup flour

1½ teaspoon baking powder

½ teaspoon baking soda

½ teaspoon salt

1 cup milk

2 to 2¼ cup sour cherries drained — save juice for sauce

½ cup chopped nuts

Bake at 350º for 50 minutes

Serve with hot sauce on top of baked cake.

Hot Sauce (use can of cherries packed in its own juice)

½ cup sugar

Pinch of salt

2 tablespoons cornstarch

¾ cup cherry juice

1 cup water

Cook until thick

Custard

1 can (14 ounces) sweet condensed milk

4 cups hot water

6 eggs

2 teaspoons vanilla extract

¼ teaspoon salt

Nutmeg to decorate

Preheat oven to 325 degrees

Mix condensed milk and hot water in glass or metal bowl.

In another bowl, whisk eggs until they are light in color & fluffy to touch. Pour the hot milk mixture into eggs until they have softened, then mix them well. Add vanilla and salt. Pour into custard bowls and place on a high-sided baking tray. Or using 2-quart baking dish instead.

Place tray in oven and fill baking dish with a half-inch water. Baking for 1 hr. or to a knife comes out clean in center. If using larger baking dish, bake for

1 hr. & 40 min.

Leave the custard to cool for an hour. Sprinkling with nutmeg and serve hot or chilled.

Cherry Pie

Preheat oven to 425°

<u>Crust</u>: (traditional two crust pie crust)

In a bowl, place two cups flour and 1 teaspoon salt. Cut in with a fork or pastry blender,

⅔ cup Crisco until the size of peas.
Sprinkle with 4 tablespoons of hot water. Mix lightly with fork.

Gather dough to clean sides of bowl. Divide and press each into a ball.

Roll each out into round shape to fit the 9-inch pie plate. Only roll out once. Re-working the dough does not produce the pie dough you want. Roll out the top crust in the same way.

Fill the lined pastry with the cherry filling. Add the top crust.

Filling:

1 cup sugar	1 can red sour pitted cherries
¼ cup flour	1⅓ tablespoon butter or margarine
½ teaspoon cinnamon	Crust for a two crust 9-inch pie

Combine sugar, flour, cinnamon, undrained cherries in a saucepan. Cook over medium heat, stirring constantly, until mixture thickens and come to a boil. About 7 minutes. Remove from heat. Pour into 9-inch pastry lined pie pan. Dot with the butter. Cover with the top crust, seal edges, and crimp. With a sharp knife, cute six holes in the top or create an artful opening.

Bake at 425° for 30-35 minutes, or until nicely browned and juice bubbles through openings crust. Serve warm. Makes 6-8 servings.

Other Books by Doris Gaines Rapp

Fiction

Honeysuckle Rose

The Boy with the Golden Horn

Tucker's Perfect Day

The Many Lives of Tucker McBride

Tucker McBride

Length of Days Trilogy

Just in Time

News at Eleven

Escape from the Shadows

Escape from the Belfry

Hiawassee – Child of the Meadow

Smoke from Distant Fires

Length of Days – Search for Freedom

Length of Days – Beyond the Valley of the Keepers

Length of Days – The Age of Silence

Non-Fiction

A Man of Significance

Pray Them to Heaven

Promote Yourself

Prayer Therapy of Jesus

Waiting for Jesus in a Can't Wait World – Advent 2014

ABOUT THE AUTHOR

Doris Gaines Rapp, Ph.D. is an author, psychologist, educator, and speaker. Her books are loved by all those who read them. Doris enjoys painting and drawing, including the covers of three of her books and the interior pages of one. She has spoken before many groups, has sung for many others, and has written songs she shares. Rapp has led spiritual retreats. She has begun speaking on her 7th great-grandfather, John Gowen.

While still a full-time psychologist, Doris directed the counseling centers at Taylor University, in Upland, Indiana, and then Bethel University, Mishawaka, Indiana. She has taught undergraduate and graduate courses in psychology at local universities. Rapp taught a graduate course in Counseling at the Caribbean Graduate School of Theology in Kingston, Jamaica.

Doris and her husband, Bill, reared six children. Now that they are grown, Doris and Bill enjoy their small-town life. She loves the stories that come to her, and Bill still serves as a pastor and Chaplain. Dr. Rapp's desire for all of you — "I hope you live all of your life."